The Fabulous Family

Hölömöläiset

The Fabulous Family *Hölömöläiset*

A Minnesota Finnish Family's Oral Tradition

by
Patricia Eilola

NORTH STAR PRESS OF ST. CLOUD, INC.

Dedication

To Daddy (Clifford Emil Johnson),
whose loving kindness engendered "Pa";
To Mom (Marion Elmi Brosie Johnson),
whose courage transcended the pain;
and for
Mary, Katy, Erick, and Kelsey,
who inherit their spirit . . .
and ours . . .
with all our love,
Little Gramma, the dreamer,
and
Papa, the dream catcher

Library of Congress Cataloging-in-Publication Data

Eilola, Patricia, 1937-
    The fabulous family Holomolaiset : A Minnesota Finnish family's
oral tradition / by Patricia Eilola.
    128 p. 23 cm.
    ISBN 0-87839-108-8 (pbk.)
    1. Finns—Minnesota—History—Fiction. 2. Pioneers—Minnesota—
Fiction. 3. Minnesota—Social life and customs—Fiction.
4. Frontier and pioneer life—Minnesota—Fiction. 5. Family—Minnesota—
Fiction. I. Title.
PS3555.I45F33 1996
813´.54--dc20   96-27925
                                                                                CIP

Cover design by Don Bruno

Illustrated by Corinne A. Dwyer

Copyright © 1996 Patricia Eilola

ISBN: 0-87839-108-8

Printed in the United States of America by Versa Press, Inc., of East Peoria, Illinois.

Published by:
    North Star Press of St. Cloud, Inc.
    P.O. Box 451
    St. Cloud, Minnesota 56302

Preface

IN HER LATER YEARS, during the winter, Gramma Jenny sat for hours near the kitchen wood stove, using oversized shears to cut carpet rags of old shirts and dresses, blouses and linens. The long, thin strips were then sewn together, end to end, on her pedal-operated White sewing machine, and wound into balls.

Grampa Alfred set up Gramma's wooden loom in the sun porch where she moved on long, hot summer afternoons to weave rag rugs, which now, fifty years later, still soften our wooden floors.

After Saturday night sauna, the family—my parents and my aunts and uncles—sat around the kitchen table talking, reminiscing, also weaving . . . tales. Their words, warm as wood smoke, drifted up through the heat register to Gramma's bedroom, where my cousins and I crouched, listening, especially to the secret parts, always told in Finn.

Within each chapter of this book, the frame story centers on the lives of a Finnish immigrant family like our own, with a mother (Äiti) and father (Isä) and their children, one of whom was my dad, through whose voice Pa attempts to speak. Daddy, too, was a gentle teller of tales. Thus many of the peripheral characters, such as Lehti Aapo, Suutari Erkki, and Kastren Papa really existed, though their character interpretations are my own. The incentive action of the story is also true, although it was not Tonttu who hurt Verner; it was my uncle who tried to do that to my dad. What happened in the frame story by and large really happened but not necessarily to the character described in the way described.

My husband, the dream catcher, says I have woven the lives of the people I care about, all through the book. He is right. The frame story just grew and grew, the characters as real to me and as precious as the people whose lives they represent.

I am not sure where or how I first heard of the Hölömöläiset. It is certain that the tales of such a fabulous family existed in the minds of both generations of Finnish immigrants—my grandparents and my parents. Always, in the stories, the Hölömöläiset—whether they faced the perils of the pirates or the stealth of the giant Stallo or the traumas of cold and hunger—emerged gloriously victorious.

Some of the tales were familiar to me before I began; some I spun myself, as I did the frame sequence, from threads of reminiscence like the rugs my gramma wove.

Central to the text is the concept of family—of the Hölömöläiset family, which survived, and of the immigrant families, which endured as they too faced hunger and cold, peril and pain.

The story is, therefore, a tale within a tale within a tale—of Äiti and Isä rerooting the legends of their homeland, of the narrator unpacking the secrets of the leather-bound trunk, of the writer working them all into a circle ending where it began, in a past that may have been.

Listeners do not have to be Finnish to resonate to the story. As the lives of the Hölömöläiset and the immigrants, tested so often by tragedy, were ultimately illumined or destroyed by the truth, so truth forms a core of any family's survival in any society at any time.

That is the tale within which these tales are told.

That it is or is not factual seems less important than that it is true, true to the memory of the spirits now resting in the cemetery on the hill but woven still into the pattern of our lives.

Patricia Eilola

Contents

Chapter 1

"Lauantai"
A Saturday without Company

THE VARIOUS VOICES OF THE WIND murmured, cried, groaned and howled 'round the sturdy log walls of our homestead cabin. It was winter, pioneer winter in the wooded lands of northern Minnesota, and the blizzard had lasted for days.

"Make the wind stop," Maija-Liisa demanded.

Äiti answered quietly, "Soon it will be over," as she went about her work baking fresh *rieska* and cutting up potatoes for *mojakka*.

The days were long—the rhythm of life disturbed—the trails so snow-bleached that even though it was Saturday no one could come visiting.

But after supper the evenings sped by, for *Isä* threw a birch log into the *kakluuni*, lighted his pipe, and leaned back in the rocking chair that *Äiti* had brought all the way from Finland. That was the signal for *Äiti* to bring out her knitting and for us to curl up on the hearth in a heavy woolen quilt and listen with serious intent to the tales *Isä* told us, tales of wonder and adventure and mystery.

As the firelight flickered, we always begged, "One more story, please, please, *Isä!*"

And it was always a story about the fabulous family called the Hölömöläiset. As Sami people, these Lapland Finns traveled all through the summer, traversing the tundra, following the reindeer to their grazing places.

☽ ○ ✳ ○ ☾

IN LATE AUTUMN IN FINLAND [*Isä began*], the sky is dark, heralding the season of snow. Pine trees touch the moon. Birch and poplar wave lullabies. The lakes rest, calm and still. Deer nestle under boughs of fragrant cedar, and the country awaits the coming of the North Wind.

1

[*Maija-Liisa giggled in anticipation, pushing her felted shoe packs close to my legs. She was always cold, snuggling against me, the corner of the quilt in her mouth.*]

One day when the rabbits had turned from brown to gray and the trees had already begun to sing the song of winter, Mummu Hölömöläinen lost her temper. She shifted Baby Vieno to her left hip and flipped the whip over the heads of the reindeer. The wagon bounced.

"Now, Father Jussi," she said to her husband, "it be time to find our winter dwelling place. If we don't stop soon, we be snowed in on the road like last year."

Overhearing her, Ahti shivered. He could remember their last winter. It had been long. It had been cold in the wagon, and crowded. He had been hungry.

"Ya, ya. I know, Mummu. But first we got'ta get some food." Father Jussi's voice was deep and low. His children thought it came from his toes, and sometimes at night they sneaked to see if the toes had mouths. They had never found any, but still. . . . "Now, poys," his voice rolled, "you quit dat yumping an' go see if there be a lake here some b'lace."

Silence.

"Poys! *Tule tänne.* Come here!" When Father Jussi's voice deepened to that thunderous roar, they all knew they had better obey.

So from the back of the wagon, from the treetops, from the wooded sides of the road they came:

[*Singing the litany, Maija-Liisa and I recited their names with Isä.*]
First Eino the oldest,
then Urho and Matti,
then Toivo and Sulo, the twins,
Onnie, Pekka, and Kalle,
and Ahti, the sailor,
and Severi, last of those Finns.

"Girls, *tyttö*, you, too!" Father Jussi's thundery rumble stopped the reindeer in their tracks, and out of the wagon jumped Liisa and Toini and Suoma and Hilja and . . . and . . .

[*Isä paused. "And . . .," he prompted, "and . . ."*

"And Florida!" Maija-Liisa crowed triumphantly, earning three approving looks.]

And Florida. Fifteen of the sixteen Hölömöläiset children gathered politely into a semi-circle to hear what their father had to say.

"Winter be almos' here," Father Jussi began, "an' it be time for us to fin' a b'lace to live. You go now. Walk in front of da wagon and watch f'r a lake. There we find *vetta*, water. There we build a house. There we catch some fish."

The children did as they were told, and the wagon wound slowly along the forest trail. The sky darkened gradually to a threatening mauve-black. The wind slipped the cover off the wagon and harried the reindeer.

The children walked and walked and looked and looked.

Just before dusk, Eino rounded a bend. "*Tule! Tule!* Come!" he yelled. "Here be a lake!"

"*Missä?* Where?" cried Toivo, running with Sulo toward the sound of Eino's voice. "Where?" Sulo echoed.

Before them, near a grove of virgin pine, the land sloped and curved, encircling a storm-tossed lake.

"Father Jussi! Father Jussi!" they hollered.

Father Jussi lashed the reindeer, and the wagon lurched to the edge of the lake where the whole family lined up to formulate a plan.

"Mummu," asked Ahti, pulling on her skirts, "how we gonna get dem fish? No time to string poles."

Ahti understood the ways of the waters. Not for nothing had he been named for the king of the waves.

Father Jussi said, "Oh, oh."

The children hunkered down.

Father Jussi thought for a long while, pulling at his gray beard. Then his head came up, his eyes brightened, and he barked, "Eino, take Toivo, Sulo, and Onnie. You poys go dig worms. Pekka, Kalle, Severi, you take birch bark an' make baskets an' catch as many flies as you can. You girls, you go empty da wagon. An' Ahti, you stan' by da lake an' sing dem waves to sleep. We gonna get dem fish."

Everybody ran.

Soon the wagon was empty, and Father Jussi pulled it even closer to the lake. The boys filled the bottom with worms and flies then stationed themselves as Father Jussi directed all around the edge of the cove, calling . . .

"Here fish, fish, fish! Wagon's fulla worms. Winter's comin' soon! Come get-cher food!"

They called and called, pleading, cajoling, until slowly, slowly silvery streaks slipped through the gray, and symmetrical shapes swam toward shore.

"Hurry now, Eino," Father Jussi whispered. "Get dem reindeer goin' soon as I holler."

Eino crept stealthily to the front of the wagon.

Slowly, the fish gathered at the shore.

All of the children from Urho to Florida lay flat on the ground very, very quietly waiting . . . waiting . . . until one by one the fish jumped into the back of the wagon and began to gobble up the worms and flies.

More and more vaulted up, leap-fishing over each other, until finally the wagon was full.

Father Jussi roared, "O.K., Eino!"

The wagon moved forward slowly at first, then faster and faster away from the shore.

Some of the fish jumped out right away, but most of them were too full to move.

So the Hölömöläiset got their winter stores.

"*Hyvä, hyvä!* Good!" I clapped.

Äiti held a finger to her lips, murmuring "Shhh." Maija-Liisa had fallen asleep. *Äiti* carried her to our bed and nestled her between the flannel sheets.

Isä reached for me.

The fire crackled in the stillness, a popple log sparking its own approval.

Isä, too, held a finger to his lips and wrapped me into the quilt. But instead of following *Äiti,* he carried me toward the door. We slipped outside, just the two of us, into the stillness.

Everywhere we looked lay snow. The air—clear, crisp and clean—crackled like the fire. The wind had carried the clouds away, and in their wake drifted the moon, lightly dusted with the treetop's brush of white.

The earth around us was alight. Along the fringes of the forest where the wolves often howled, an icy brilliance highlighted the trees, shadowing their branches on the snow. Sharp as wolves' teeth close to their trunks, the branches blurred into feather fronds of ferns reaching toward us, softly furred.

I gasped. My breath, caught in grayish tentacles, turned milky white in the moonglow and froze there as the moment did with me in my *Isä's* arms.

Isä's heart beat against mine as we slipped back inside. His moustache brushed my cheek.

Only *Äiti* and *Isä* and Maija-Liisa and I lived in our house, snugly warm under the trees, our root cellar replete with harvest from garden and woods.

Storm winds gone, sleep would come, as would morning through the quiet, gentle night.

Tomorrow the rhythm of our daily lives would return.

Tomorrow we could see our neighbors again.

And tomorrow perhaps the Hölömöläiset, too, would build a safe winter home.

I did not know, of course, that few of those hopes would come true.

Chapter 2

"Sunnuntai"

A Sunday without Church

AND, AS IT TURNED OUT, for one reason or another, the Hölömöläiset (and I) did have to wait.

By morning, all that remained of the storm was the snow, windblown into every crevice, piled against every impediment. The northeast walls of the sauna and barn had acted as snow fences protecting the house from the worst of the drifts. Still, Isä and Äiti spent that entire day shoveling, carving narrow pathways through swooping curves of white, in the process creating a winter maze for Maija-Liisa and me.

Maija-Liisa, too short to see over the edges of the paths, considered them her province, and that too had its advantages. When we went outside, Äiti usually had to remind me that, since I was older, I was responsible for keeping an eye on Maija-Liisa every minute. That Sunday I was absolved. Maija-Liisa had an outside playpen with walls, and I was free to play. I built a house out of chunks of snow, furnished it with wood from the woodshed and decorated it with scraps from Äiti's quilting bag, which I promised to return.

Isä shook his head at the weather. Storms were usually followed by arctic cold. Then, housebound for fear of frostbite, we drew patterns on window panes covered with filagree frost as lacy as the tatting on our good dresses and on the pillowcases we saved for best.

But all through this tranquil, happy day, the last day of my childhood, a radiance of sun and snow sparkled. The pine trees cast shadows far bluer than the crisp robin's-egg sky, and icicles dripped spring rhythm from the eaves.

In the afternoon Isä carried armloads of wood to replenish the woodboxes inside of the sauna and in the back lean-to porch and hauled pail after pail of water from the artesian spring that gushed in winter as in summer from a pipe he had stuck into the side of the hill at the edge of the woods. It had been one reason that he had chosen this land to homestead, for Äiti was always scrubbing and cleaning our house and the sauna and our clothes and us.

Warmed by the smile of the Sunday sun, the snow gradually settled, until its moisture rose like cream that I pressed into white butterballs. Isä stopped to help me lift small ones onto larger ones until I had an entire snow family—an Isä, an Äiti, and two girls to inhabit the house and play with me.

We had no horse and cutter to skim over the snow, and Isä and Äiti were hesitant to ski even the two-mile path to the Makelas, unwilling to leave our home fires unattended even for a short time after so severe a storm.

In truth, visits to the Makelas were a mixed blessing. I enjoyed playing with the five Makela girls, but Äiti shook her head about their house, which wasn't very clean even during the summer. Unlike Isä, Mr. Makela, though entertaining and kind, was not a worker. He did not stock the woodshed every fall; he did not split and pile wood. He just dumped the logs in a heap near the kitchen door. The Makela girls had to push a whole log bit by bit into the stove, leaving the outside door partly open and allowing the smoke to escape. In the winter, their whole house smelled like a *noki sauna*, a smoke sauna, which had no chimney but only a high window through which the smoke escaped. No stove pipe led from the sauna *kiuas* up through a chimney as it did in ours.

When we did go to the Makelas for a Saturday night sauna visit, our eyes burned. Usually we bathed again when we got home.

On winter sauna nights, Isä filled not only the water storage tank built into the side of the heavy metal fire box, the *kiuas*, but also the big square wash-tubs Äiti used on Mondays to soak and wash our clothes. After we had washed and rinsed our bodies and our hair squeaky clean, we sat on the bottom step of the three-level wooden benches we called *lavat* to watch Isä unbraid, wash, and rinse Äiti's thick brown hair, so long it touched the back of her knees when she stood, so long it fell from the top *lavat* all the way down to where we sat when she lay supine for its washing.

Steam-cleaned and scrubbed inside and out, bundled into fleece-lined woolen long underwear and thick gray shoe packs, we raced into the house, too warm to need coats, there to watch entranced as Isä combed and brushed Äiti's copper strands until they rivaled the glint of the sand-scoured tea kettle on the back burner of our black cookstove.

Then as a special treat, we drank milk-coffee from heavy white mugs, pouring it into our saucers as Isä did and sipping it through sugar lumps held between our teeth. Äiti always cut the last of the week's bread into thick fingers, sprinkled it with cinnamon-sugar and toasted it until the strips were crispy enough to hold their shapes even when dunked into the coffee. I slathered mine with butter.

On nights like that even the Hölömöläiset seemed redundant, peripheral to the warm center of our lives.

But then the news came.

Äiti always warned us that life follows cycles like the weather, that as sunshine follows storms, so too often storms follow sunshine.

The storm struck when Kastren-Papa knocked on the door and walked in, wearing his long black coat and black hat, carrying his doctor's bag.

The summer before, he had appeared out of nowhere just when Äiti needed him. Maija-Liisa had suddenly begun to have nosebleeds so heavy and frequent that even touching her nose caused it to bleed. Nothing in our Sodergren medicine cabinet did any good. Äiti was worried. The word was passed along.

Kastren-Papa, famous for his ointments and herbal medicines, told Äiti, "I will fix medicine to stop that bleeding." Then he went behind the sauna and did. The potion he mixed made Maija-Liisa throw up, but it cured the nosebleeds. She might have thrown up anyway because she was afraid of him.

I hated to admit it because I was older, but I was frightened of him, too. He had been knifed in Finland and lost one eye; the glass replacement never closed. Even when he slept on the floor in front of the fire, it looked at us. Maija-Liisa would have preferred the nosebleeds.

That Sunday night, Kastren-Papa was on his way to a lumber camp near the spur railroad track the Rainy Lake Mill had run from Leander to Jacksons' stone and timber claim, not far beyond Makelas. One of the *jibbos* had fallen from a high load of logs onto the iced horse track.

The word had been passed along.

We had expected that Isä would go to that logging camp to work as soon as we could spare him.

Instead, he got the word from Kastren-Papa. The underground mine in Soudan was hiring.

We needed the money, Äiti and Isä carefully explained. Although our homestead land had been free and Isä had cut the logs for the buildings when he cleared our fields, although Äiti had packed rutabagas and carrots and potatoes into the root cellar for the winter and canned as much venison as she had jars left from blueberry and raspberry sauce, although she made all of our clothes, even spinning yarn for mittens and soaking and shaping bats of wool for the warm *tossut* pushed into our winter boots when we went outside and wore like slippers inside, even though they had tried very hard not to spend a penny more than they absolutely had to on crackers and apples and winter supplies, even though . . .

We got the message.

We needed our own horse, we needed chickens to replace the ones the brush wolves had eaten, we needed a pig so we could smoke bacon and hams and render lard, we needed seeds for the garden.

The mines paid well.

They showed us Isä's brown leather pouch, virtually empty.

We had left Soudan because Isä hated the mine, hated climbing into the iron cage that clanked down to a cold black tomb, where he spent days of death in life, leaving too early to see the sunrise, clanking back up, red-brown with ore that Äiti had trouble getting off of his clothes, in the darkness of the early night.

Isä's eyes, usually as deep blue as the shadowed snow, turned storm gray in times of trouble or when he talked or thought of the mine.

But mining paid much better than lumberjack wages.

We knew we could not go with him. He would make arrangements for Lehti Aapo to stay with us as was the pattern during haymaking. Lehti Aapo didn't mind sleeping in the sauna, which was bigger than his shack on *Tupun Kallio* and a lot cleaner. Äiti would de-louse him and his clothes; she would feed him well and forebear from lectures. He liked Äiti, called her "Yenni" and tried hard to stay sober.

Isä would ski the twenty-three miles to Soudan, stay there in the *poika- talo* boarding house and ski home every Sunday he was free.

We knew the wolves would trail him, coming and going, never at his heels, but close, always close, yipping and howling. Even the foot-thick log walls of the house could not shield us from their pack meetings or from the screams that sometimes preceded an ensuing silence.

Isä buried a deer carcass behind the barn. Wolves had picked it clean.

I shuddered when I thought of him alone on his gray wooden skis.

And then I remembered the Hölömöläiset. Before Isä left, it seemed important to get them to a place of safety.

And so, after Kastren-Papa was settled in the sauna, on that last night together, although I knew I should go to sleep to allow Äiti a chance to cry with- out upsetting Maija-Liisa or me, I pretended I was a baby again. I climbed onto Isä's lap and took a deep breath of his shaving soap and of the faint hint of wood smoke that clung to his hair after he stoked the fires, banking them care- fully for the night. "Please, Isä," I begged, "one story, please. Tell us how the Hölömöläiset got their winter home."

Äiti held Maija-Liisa instead of knitting; they listened too.

The logs cracked, and we were gone . . . back to Finland to the land of the reindeer people, among whom lived the fabulous family Isä called the Hölömöläiset.

THE FIRST NIGHT NEAR THE LAKE WAS VERY COLD. Father Jussi's beard froze, Baby Vieno had to thaw the tears she cried (she was always crying), and the boys huddled together under the wagon, filled now with fish.

Eino woke up just as the sun announced the morning with a pink and orange banner. "*No voi*, it be cold! Whooosh!" he cried, jumping up and down until he got his blood moving again. He laughed at Father Jussi's beard, which made him look like *Joulu Pukki*, the Christmas elf, ate the fish Mummu chopped into pieces, and ran into the woods to find the reindeer, which had wandered away during the night. Switching them into line, he hurried back. As soon as everyone was awake and breakfast over, Father Jussi divulged his plan for the day: on this day Mummu and the girls were to smoke and salt the fish; the boys to build the house. Only five logs were needed—one for each side and one for beams for the roof.

[*Trees are bigger in Finland, Isä explained to our wide eyes.*]

Father Jussi set up a system for cutting the logs. First, Ahti climbed to the top of the tree to fasten a rope. Ahti always pretended the trees were the masts of sailing ships and he a sailor. Then Father Jussi walked backwards from the tree in the direction he wanted it to fall, gauged its height, and marked a line with his boot where the topmost tip would land. It was Onnie's job to chop the directional mark on the front of the tree—he was the best woodsman—and Eino's job to stand on the other side and push—he was the biggest—while all of the other boys pulled on the rope until the tree began to fall.

Father Jussi's deep base voice resonated, "TIMMMBBBEERR!"

The tree dropped, jarring Mother Earth until she echoed Father Jussi's cry. As the soft tips of the top pine needles brushed Father Jussi's line, all was quiet again.

Jumping up onto the trunk of the fallen tree, the boys hacked off the large branches and cracked off the small ones. The girls took these to fuel the smoke-barrel.

Mummu filled Baby Vieno's *kamse* made of birch branches and reindeer skin with a soft pile of pine needles, tucked her inside, and hung the cradle from a low sturdy branch so she could concentrate on her job, scraping off the pitch she would use to stop the bleeding when the boys hurt themselves.

It took one day to fell each tree. Every one of the boys, working together, dragged them into a square and hewed the corners until they fit together snugly. The reindeer had to help with making the roof.

[*"How?" Maija-Liisa interrupted.*]

The oldest boy, Eino, made a ramp on one side of the wall of log, tied a rope to the reindeer's huge antlers and led the reindeer to the outside of the opposite wall. When he yelled "Pull!" the reindeer pulled so hard that the log rolled up the ramp and onto the log walls, putting the roof beams right in place.

"I don't believe it," I said, skeptically. We had tried to train Makelas' horse to obey commands the summer before, and he had balked, just standing there, not moving, not pulling the hay wagon or doing one thing but looking at us with his head down. Isä and Mr. Makela had had to pull the haywagon themselves. Even the offers of a carrot and a sugar lump had failed. He was one dumb, lazy horse. Were reindeer really that much more . . . tractable? It seemed unlikely.

"Reindeer will pull anything," Isä affirmed, "even the sleigh Santa used on Christmas Eve. Remember?"

We nodded. We remembered. Well, I remembered. Maija-Liisa pretended she did, too. We had heard the bells on the cutter/sleigh on Christmas Eve. At first it had sounded as if the bells were going right by, and I had shivered in bed, remembering the many times I had not been responsible even though I was older. I feared that this American innovation—Santa Claus, a friend of *Joulu Pukki's*—had missed our house and gone to Makelas', and that there would be no presents now or later, as they appeared in Finland, in our shoes at the foot of the bed or in the stockings on the *kakluuni* when we woke up in the morning.

Then the jingling on the harness had grown louder and louder again. Isä and Äiti had made us put our heads under our pillows while they went out to see what Santa and his reindeer team had brought. It could have been coal or sticks. I was not always responsible even though I was older.

But when they came in, we each had received a stick of peppermint candy, an orange that we saved and devoured bit by bit, even the rind, and one bright shiny copper penny.

And in the morning we had found reindeer prints in the snow.

Joulu Pukki, too, had slipped in during the night, leaving each of us a pair of brand new mittens, Maija-Liisa's blue, mine red, with matching scarves; a cradle that Isä had helped him carve for our wooden dolls and a new dress for each of them that Äiti had helped to make; and, unbelievably, two long black ropes of licorice candy, our favorite, something neither Äiti nor Isä ever bought. We didn't have the money.

The Hölömöläiset reindeer hypothesis had not seemed sound, but memories of Christmas past established probability, and I settled back, placated. Isä continued with the story:

THE BOYS AND THE GIRLS ALL WORKED HARD for five days until the fish and the house were ready for inspection.

Mummu and Father Jussi smiled. "*Hyvä. Hyvä.* Good. Good," they murmured as they tasted the fish, some of it salted instead of smoked.

"Mmmm," the boys agreed.

"*Hyvä. Hyvä.* Good. Good," Father Jussi and Mummu said, nodding as they walked around the log house, around to the other side, around to the . . . to . . . the . . .

"*Minä sanon etta joku on hullu!*" Father Jussi's roar split another tree right in half and terrified the waves into covering an island they had been forming in the center of the lake. "I be telling for you someone be crazy!"

In a whisper as ominous as the first snowflake of a blizzard or the soft rustling breezes of a northeasterly gale, Father Jussi said, "Where . . . be . . . the . . . door?"

"It's . . . it's . . . we forgot it!" The boys, terrified too, began to run—most of them into the woods, one or two into the lake, swimming all the way across before they could stop. Eino was so afraid, he did not even watch where he was going. *Wham!* Eino ran right through the wall.

"Ouch!" cried Eino.

Thus Father Jussi got his door. And Mummu used the pitch for the first time that winter.

[*Maija-Liisa giggled. "But he didn't really hurt himself, did he?" she asked.*

"No, not at all," Isä agreed. "Eino's head was tougher than any log in the forest."]

"Tyttö, girls, you cover that door with reindeer skin for the night," Mummu ordered as they crawled in through the Eino-shaped opening.

Every visitor they had that winter wondered why the door looked just like Eino. All in all, he was pretty proud.

"Did they have windows like ours?" I asked. Not only did we have windows, we had glass in them. Isä had had to haul that glass carefully from Soudan the summer before, and I was a bit smug about it. Makelas didn't have glass windows yet.

"Well . . . that's another story," drawled Isä in a voice as quiet as Father Jussi's whisper. He motioned toward the rocker. This time Äiti and Maija-Liisa had both fallen asleep.

Soon I would be sleeping, too. But for just a little while I was glad to sit there quietly, cuddled in Isä's lap, safe and warm. I could wait for the Hölömöläiset to get their windows until Isä came back from Soudan, and I would hold them . . . and him . . . safe and warm in my heart until he did.

🌙 ○ ✴ ○ ☾

Chapter 3

"Maanantai"
Monday Washday

WHEN I AWOKE, Äiti's determinedly cheerful voice and the empty coat hook by the door confirmed what the silence of the house had shouted: Isä was gone.

I ran to the door and opened it to a flurry of white. Double narrow indentations, the trail of his skis, were already sifting in with snow, like flour on a bread board.

He was gone, and it was too late to find answers to the questions that had awakened me so soon after dawn.

One was a persistent concern about the Hölömöläiset's windows. To live in the dark would be to live like a mole. I shuddered. Trips to the root cellar for potatoes or jars of berries or canned venison had always been trips into a nightmare for me, a waking dream of being stifled, covered, enclosed in earth.

Once the previous summer when the sky had turned mauve black after a scorching, heavy, air-less day, Isä had come running in from the fields with his hoe still in hand and sweat dripping from his face to push and pull and virtually carry us into that storage place shoveled into the hill and roofed with sod.

"A tornado's coming!" he had yelled. "Run for the root cellar!"

He lowered a heavy board into the slots to secure the door behind us; and we cowered together in the bleak blackness, listening to the howl of wind, louder and more frightening even than the wolves.

The Makelas, who had driven their wagon to Lake Leander that morning to fish and hunt for berries, had hidden under the wagon when the winds came and feared for their lives as trees crashed down around them, roots flailing the air like the arms of prisoners helpless in the face of Russian attack during the White War. Then the lake had risen as if a hand had lifted it or as if the earth itself had heaved and vomited water so that it came at them in a rushing wave.

The Makalas had only been bruised, but they had lost their wagon, splintered above them by the three-pronged attack of wind, water, and falling trees. Even worse, their horse Prince, leaping and rearing at the sound of the wind, had impaled himself on the wagon pole.

It had been a disastrous loss. A horse made the difference between plowing a garden plot and plowing maybe twenty acres of the homestead. It meant the difference between getting to the Soudan hospital in time or dying as Mr. Victormaki's first wife had with her newborn baby in her arms.

I knew we were lucky to be safe in the root cellar. I knew I should bless its stout earthen walls and heavy barred door. But when the storm was over and Isä carried me out, I could not stop shaking.

I was shaking now again, for Isä was gone. Who now could tell me how the Hölömöläiset got light into their house? Who now would tell me how the Hölömöläiset dressed so I could dress my doll correctly? Who now could explain why the deer here in Minnesota couldn't be trained like Finnish reindeer to pull a wagon and help with building instead of just being hunted for food.

I had touched a baby deer once as we walked to the blueberry patch on the Tupun Kallio hills. The fawn had lain in a glade in the forest, dappled and shy, unafraid until its mother signaled it to run.

I had wanted to assure its limpid brown eyes that it was safe with us. I had wanted Isä to understand what seemed obvious to me: he could not shoot that fawn's Isä or Äiti. Obviously he had never thought of reindeer and American deer as being cousins, relatives, *suku laisia*, of the same family, thence of a like being.

Isä and Äiti opened our door to anyone who shared not only their name and family lineage but their home country province in Finland, their *omanpaikkasia*. Surely Isä could see that reindeer and American deer also shared a similar heritage. Perhaps the American deer could become our friends and co-workers as Finnish reindeer were.

Isä would listen.

But Isä was gone.

And the matter of clothing was a matter of concern for an equally significant reason. Should some of the Hölömöläiset arrive in America and by chance at our own door, how would I know the visitors to be the Hölömöläiset if I didn't know how they dressed? Whenever I had a question of any significance, Äiti always said, "Ask Isä." Dejected, I gathered my quilt about me and padded wordlessly back to bed. I felt bereft and very much alone.

For breakfast that morning Äiti mixed an extra big glop of butter into our *puuroa*, stirring the right amount of cream into the hot cereal, a little for me because I like it thick, a lot for Maija-Liisa, who preferred it runny.

Äiti made our cereal with care so that it was never lumpy, and Äiti had her own special starter for our morning *viili*, which was thick and rich, but never stringy. That morning she opened a jar of blueberry sauce and gave us double servings without our even asking. But she paused at the stove, coffee pot in hand, and forgot to pour any into her heavy white mug.

"Maybe Kastren-Papa was wrong," she mused. "Maybe the mine isn't hiring."

"*Sattuu,*" I agreed. "May be." But neither her tone of voice nor mine expressed any real hope. They were as empty and flat as our hearts.

Thanks to Äiti's patient directions, Lehti Aapo, surrogate grandfather and *sukulainen*, whom Isä had asked Kastren-Papa to send to help us, stoked up the sauna fire, which had been banked for the night, and lifted the galvanized square wash tubs up onto their wooden bench ready for washday. The bench was high enough to keep Äiti's back from hurting as she slivered homemade lye soap into the hot water and rubbed our dirty clothes and linen against the washboard.

On washday Äiti had a system, and Maija-Liisa and I had our jobs.

After Sunday night sauna, Äiti put the white things—sheets and dish towels and underwear and rags—to boil and soak for the night.

In the morning Maija-Liisa, who was just learning her colors, put the dirty clothes and linen into piles according to colors before she was allowed to play with the wooden clothespins, whose round "heads" and divided "legs" made them seem like little dolls. Until the previous summer I also had spent washday playing with the "dolls," but Isä ended that part of my childhood freedom forcefully after the day Äiti cried.

Maija-Liisa and I had been told many times that we were not to go near the blacking jar or to touch the blacking rags Äiti used once a week to clean the stove, applying the blacking to the rags and rubbing the stove first with the rags and then with waxed paper until the stove-top gleamed.

But we had seen what the blacking did to her hands, which she had to scrub afterwards, and we were enchanted with the idea of making our faces as black as the face of the man we had seen on the street in Soudan.

Isä had insisted that he had been born that way, that he was a "Knee-Grow," but we were quite sure that the truth of the matter was tied to the blacking rag.

The morning of the episode of the blacking rag, Isä had called out for help. Dolly the cow had gotten into the garden, and it was imperative to get her out immediately but without upsetting her as she was with calf.

Äiti set the blacking rag down on the top of the jar, but in her hurry she forgot to repeat the warning, and we "forgot" to remember.

I reached for the rag first, I admit that. But Maija-Liisa did not demur. By the time Äiti got back into the house, we had applied the cloth vigorously to each other's faces and unfortunately in the process to our dresses.

The dresses, equally unfortunately, were new, pieced together by hand from an old petticoat of Äiti's, summer-light and white.

But though the material had been reused, Äiti had tatted a decorative edging on collars, cuffs, and hem. It had taken her many many nights of work, which she had assured Isä she loved doing. I had seen her at the table, bending near the kerosene lamp, our dresses-to-be in hand, hurrying to finish them because the weather had turned hot after a wet and rainy June.

Of course, Maija-Liisa could have worn my last year's pink sprigged summer cotton. But back in Finland when Äiti was little, she had been the youngest sister who had to wear the mended hand-me-downs.

Thus, when she made us new clothes, we, as Maija-Liisa said, "got them both." And they were always "the same is."

The morning of the blacking fiasco had been our first in the pristine white dresses, starched crisp and ironed.

I had managed to get almost all of the blacking from my cloth onto Maija-Liisa's face. But inexpert in her aim, she had not.

Äiti tried to wash the collar and bodice of my dress clean, rubbing it on the washboard; but when the blacking had finally disappeared, so had a part of the fabric, and the resulting hole could not, it seemed, be mended.

Later, Äiti apologized for crying. It had been hot, she said, and Dolly had eaten a number of small potato plants before Äiti had shaken her apron to get her attention and Isä had lured her away with clumps of fresh hay. The potatoes would have fed us for a week or more during the winter. Once, the winter before, potatoes had been all we had to eat.

But it had been the hole in my dress that had loosed the tears. When I saw Äiti cry, I cried too and apologized with all my heart.

But the next washday Isä told me that it was important for me to understand how hard Äiti worked; now only Maija-Liisa got to play with the clothespin dolls. Since that summer day, I had been enlisted to turn the hand wringer and to hang the clean underwear, handkerchiefs, wash cloths, and rags on lines Isä hung low enough for me to reach, both in the sauna dressing room where we hung the colored clothes on winter Mondays and outside where the white clothes went even on the coldest days.

I pushed the doll clothes-pins carefully down on the corners after I had shaken the wet clothes out so they would hang neat and straight.

Sometimes when the clothes froze before we could even shake them out, Äiti just threw them over the line so they would be sun-bleached if not dry.

The Monday that Isä left was a busier washday than normal. Äiti had had to lift Lehti Aapo's clothes with a stick and boil the bugs out before she washed them.

And, after all, even on normal Mondays, we rarely saw Isä until evening. But then he would be back from the woods to join us for Monday wash-up time in a sauna still warm from the day's work.

By wash-up time we guessed that Kastren-Papa must have been right. The mine must have been hiring. Isä had not returned.

"*Voi kauhia,*" Äiti murmured, as she served us thin pancakes.

Since Isä considered pancakes breakfast food and meat and potatoes a requirement at supper time, a pancake supper should have been a treat But it was not. Instead, the reversal of menus seemed awry and out of sync and our house as dark as the Hölömöläiset cabin.

Lehti Aapo, sitting on Isä's stool at the head of the table, a courtesy seating we understood but resented, took a deep drag of his pipe.

Regardless of the pancakes, we felt empty. There would be no evening cuddle in the rocking chair for Maija-Liisa. Lehti Aapo, unaware that it was Isä's spot, had moved there. There would be no evening story.

Silently, we went behind the curtain, slipped out of our dresses, hung them neatly on the hooks by our bed, and pulled our flannel nightgowns over our heads and down.

I untied my braids, folded my ribbons neatly, and helped Maija-Liisa with hers so that Äiti could give us each the prescribed one hundred healthy-hair brushings. We took turns sitting in front of her on the stool, Maija-Liisa first. She was usually a chatterbox although sometimes it was hard to decipher what she was chattering about. That night even she was quiet, and Äiti tucked her in right away, punctuating her prayers with kisses.

Then I took my turn sitting with my back to Äiti, my face toward the fire, until without warning, the silence spilled from my soul, wet streaks of it coursing down my cheeks to dry from the heat of the fire and be replaced and dry again.

That night it was I whom Äiti pulled onto her lap, holding me with my back against her, carefully not looking at my tears.

Lehti Aapo got up, lifted a stove lid, and tapped his pipe against the edge to empty the last ashes before he nodded good night at us, pulled on his jacket and boots, and slipped quietly out the door to check the barn one last time. He would roll out a quilt in the sauna dressing room.

"Things will look brighter tomorrow," Äiti whispered in my ear. "We'll put a stick of wood by the door every morning, and when we have counted seven sticks, we'll know we can start waiting for him to come home. What a nice surprise that'll be for him to have an armload of wood ready to bring in!"

I sighed. Morning seemed far away; darkness lurked in every corner.

But warm front and back, I did address the lesser of my concerns. "How could the Hölömöläiset know when morning came if they didn't have any windows?" Perhaps there was a small chance that, like Isä, Äiti would know the answer.

"That's another story," she began, then paused, waiting for some signal that I would accept her attempt to fill Isä's role.

I cuddled back harder, adhering.

"Do you remember," she began, "when Eino ran through the wall of the cabin to make the door?"

"He didn't do it intentionally," I amended.

"Of course not. But he did make the door nonetheless, and Mummu Hölömöläinen covered it with a reindeer skin for the night."

"I remember."

"Well . . .," she continued rather hesitantly, "soon everyone was fast asleep and snug in the stout little cabin."

Outside, morning came. Baby Vieno awoke, but it was so dark inside the cabin that she went right back to sleep. Father Jussi tossed and turned and wondered why the night was lasting so long. Mummu suffered pangs of hunger, but she told herself to be patient and wait until sunrise. The rest of the children, tired from building the cabin and smoking the fish, slept on. Outside, the afternoon, too, went to rest.

Before the sun set, it wrinkled its brow as it dipped down past the rim of the lake. "Where," it thought, "are the Hölömöläiset?"

The next morning, seeing the yard still empty, the sun sent a worker beam toward a tiny crack between the logs to see what was wrong. Father Jussi got up about that same time, very hungry, but everyone else was still asleep.

"Now where be dat sun," he wondered. Then he caught glimpse of the tentacle of light poking its way between the chinks, anticipating wrath at the intrusion.

Sure enough, Father Jussi was angry. "Where you been so long?" he roared at the sunbeam, shaking his fist.

He bellowed so loudly that even the air rushed away, pushing back the heavy reindeer skin from the door and billowing out.

Frightened by the thunderous boom, the sun hid behind a cloud.

But Father Jussi knew it was morning, and he was *hungry!*

"*Tyttö*," rumbled his stomach and his voice. "Girls! You wake up, take da burlap bags and stuff 'em full a sunshine. *Right now!* We gotta get some light."

Äiti had trouble doing a Jussi voice any time, but it was especially hard when when she had to make sure she didn't wake up Maija-Liisa. She was obviously trying hard, however, so I tried, too, to get into the spirit of the story. "Did the house get full of light?" It was a rhetorical question. Of course it did. That was the way of the Hölömöläiset.

But Äiti surprised me. "No," she admitted.

"Why not?" I asked, my interest piqued. This was a twist.

"Perhaps the sun was angry with Father Jussi because he had shouted so loudly and punished him by hiding all the beams away. Or perhaps the burlap sacks leaked."

I paused to consider that one. Both alternatives offered interesting options. I liked the idea of the sun's getting back at Father Jussi, who was loud and crabby and full of orders, not at all like Isä. I could imagine him sleeping in the wagon while his sons built their winter cabin. He was even lazier than Mr. Makela.

And it was also true that burlap leaked. When Isä hauled a sack of potatoes in from the root cellar, we had to be careful where we set it down so we didn't get dirt all over the floor.

"But whatever the reason," Äiti concluded, "no matter how hard they tried, the girls could not manage to bring the sunbeams inside."

"Oh, dear," I thought, facing the possibility that the Hölömöläiset would have to spend their days as well as nights in darkness. I knew if Isä had been home, he could have solved their problem.

Unexpectedly, Äiti came to the rescue. "They did get light, though."

"How?" I asked, mollified and considerably relieved.

WHEN THE GIRLS AWOKE Eino with their running back and forth, he was so hungry that he was crabby, and he kicked out his legs as he jumped up. One of his legs hit Matti, who woke up crabby and hungry, too. The two began to fight.

Before Father Jussi or Mummu could intervene, Eino had thrown his ax at Matti. Matti threw his back, and then the other boys jumped into the fray, axes ready.

$$☽ ○ ☀ ○ ☾$$

"Oh, no!" I tried to sound appalled. I had never been allowed to touch Isä's ax because it was so very sharp, thence delightfully dangerous. But I had tried it once . . . surreptitiously, of course. It had cut my finger just a little. Oh, how exciting it would be to see it thrown so hard it stuck in the wall! Isä could do that. If he tried, he could throw it so hard that it would. . . . The image was enthralling: I could envision exactly how the Hölömöläiset got both windows and light.

"Then did the sun allow the worker beams to go in through the ax holes?" Father Jussi had been nasty, and the sun might be required to punish misdeeds just as Äiti and Isä were. When we were naughty, they had to withhold privileges: whatever we had wanted we were certain not to get.

"Not at first." Äiti, an expert at withholding privileges, understood the sun's point of view. "But finally things calmed down. The boys were sorry and put their axes away where they belonged. Father Jussi quit hollering. He may even have apologized."

"Unlikely," I thought.

"Or maybe the sun simply saw how hard the girls had been working and took pity on them. Whatever the reason, the Hölömöläiset did get enough sunshine to brighten up their house."

I nodded approvingly, and we sat in silence for a while, watching the embers glow. It was long past time for bed. But between us, Äiti and I had shared a special warmth. We cherished it for a few more minutes, nestling there together quietly.

I thought about carrying sunshine in a bag. Even in a story, it left something to be desired. Then I remembered that when Isä came back from Soudan he often carried a pack on his back, a burlap sack full of staple goods or tools or sometimes even treats. But he didn't need to fill one with sunshine to brighten up our house. All he had to do was just walk in the door.

Chapter 4

"Tiistai"

Ironing Day

On Monday we wash,
Tuesday we iron,
Wednesday we bake,
Thursday we clean,
Friday we mend,
Saturday we visit,
and on Sunday we worship.

THUS THE DAYS OF THE WEEK MARCHED to Äiti's tune. Their orderly progression, exerting control over a world fraught with disaster, served as a bulwark before which chaos usually pounded an ineffectual though still discordant drum.

Because it was Tuesday, Äiti awakened early to sprinkle and roll the starched clothes into small tight bales before she whisked us out of bed and to the table to eat our *puuroa* quickly so that she could move the circular claw-footed oak table closer to the stove. The flat irons waited hot and ready on the stovetop, and two handles stood next to the well-padded boards, one for Äiti, one for me.

Like washday Mondays, Tuesdays were no longer play-days. But I found solace in the fact that I was old enough to be Äiti's real helper, whereas Maija-Liisa had to be satisfied with a pretend iron and doll clothes that hadn't even been washed.

Äiti liked Tuesdays. Since the wood fire had to be well stoked in order to keep the flatirons hot, on winter Tuesdays the house was delightfully warm. She enjoyed, too, the act of pressing out every wrinkle before folding linens neatly in piles or hanging clothes ready for use. She did the delicate ironing— Isä's Sunday white shirt and our cotton house dresses and aprons, the tablecloth because its tatted edge caught and tore so easily. She did the heavy brushing and pressing of the woolen dresses and pants that constituted our winter wardrobes, worn on alternate weeks so as to wear out evenly.

To me were left the flat pieces, the pillow cases, four a week, seven embroidered dish towels, a clean one for each day, napkins that matched the tablecloth but lacked the tatting, four handkerchiefs per day, their edges rolled and hand stitched.

When Äiti traveled across the ocean from Finland, she did not come directly to northern Minnesota. For a time she worked for a wealthy family in Boston as a scullery maid and then, promoted, as an upstairs maid. We were aware that both she and Isä had lived other lives before they met at the logging camp in Floodwood where Äiti was cooking and Isä working, but details about those other lives were sparse, especially about the Boston experience.

It was, however, in Boston that Äiti had learned about many important things—the use of tablecloths and napkins on a regular basis, for example, and how to make an angel food cake. Because of Boston, Äiti insisted that we all dress for worship and dinner every Sunday, whether there was a church meeting or not—she in her best black wool, Isä in his wedding-and-funeral suit and shirt, and Maija-Liisa and I in shoes and dresses with lacy-crocheted collars. Because of Boston, the schedule of weekly work was indelibly ingrained. But otherwise, Boston remained a restricted subject brought up only when we questioned the way things should be done, otherwise mostly contained in the trunk.

Wealthy people packed their Finnish heritage into trunks with curved lids: the greater the curve, the wealthier the owner. Our trunk lid was flat. But that was good, Äiti said, because the trunk could then serve equally well as a bench or a table, whichever we needed more.

We knew that the trunk was full because it was difficult for us to move, even to slide it across the wooden floor boards when we scrubbed (on Thursdays, of course). But we were never allowed to delve into its contents. Never. The rule was as immutable as the parade of days. Thus the trunk's value doubled. Not only was it a trove of treasure; it was also a *secret* treasure. We remained as enthralled about its contents as we remained uninformed about Äiti's other life in Boston.

I was never allowed to put anything I ironed into the trunk. Nor, while I ironed, was I allowed to daydream about its contents, a favorite activity that usually kept me well occupied when I was doing embroidery or learning to knit or kneading bread, skills Äiti insisted I learn since I was older.

Instead of delightful daydreams about the treasures enfolded within the trunk, on ironing day, I suffered a double indignity. Not only did I have to do all of the boring flat pieces; I had to concentrate on practicing arithmetic while I was ironing.

Äiti formulated the problems: One sheet per bed plus four fresh pillowcases equals how many pieces of bedding? If we have guests on Saturday or
Sunday and use extra dish towels, how many would there be for me to iron if
the guests were, for example, the sixty thousand Victormaki children? Four
handkerchiefs per day multiplied by the four people in the family multiplied by
seven days of the week equaled how many handkerchiefs? What if one of us
had a cold and we used five extra ones two days in a row?

It didn't matter that we didn't have any extra ones. Äiti stood intransi-
gent across the table, ironing and demanding that I do sums and multiplications
in my head.

Tuesdays could have gone to perdition had I been allowed to use the
word. During church meeting—the *kahvi kekkerit*—the past summer, I had discovered it, a delightful alternative to the absolutely forbidden term I had used
once and thereafter eliminated from public use, at least where Äiti and Isä
could hear it.

Until the Tuesday of the week that Isä left for Soudan, I welcomed
and cherished any excuse to cut Tuesdays short. But after that Tuesday, I had
to admit even to myself that a day spent ironing was infinitely preferable to the
events that ensued just before Lehti Aapo came in for morning coffee.

We had just begun the regular sequence of handkerchiefs and simple
addition when the door burst open without warning. That moment will remain
frozen forever in my memory, never to thaw as the icicles do in the spring. But
it is not a frosty filagree of branches on the snow or designs on the pane. It is
an icy terror that even now makes me understand what it means to have one's
blood run cold.

In the doorway during that frozen second stood the second Mrs.
Victormaki, her son Verner in her arms. Blood dripped onto our doorsill and
froze there as it had frozen on her apron and her dress and her stockings and
on the woolen shirt she had obviously pulled on in haste and never buttoned,
as it had frozen on the pants and the shirt and the blanket with which she had
hurriedly wrapped little Verner, who was lying unmoving, almost unbreathing,
it seemed, in her arms.

Words flew to my lips but froze there, too, as she crumpled, small
child still clasped, into a heap of tears and blood and inarticulate gasping
sounds. Äiti whirled, all curving motion, to snap to me, "Get Lehti Aapo. Don't
bother with boots or coat. Run."

The very lack of exclamation in her voice emphasized her urgency far
more than a scream. Turning to obey, I compounded the trauma. For during
the second of inattention when I had focused on the second Mrs. Victormaki
and on Verner, whom I knew well since he was exactly Maija-Liisa's age and a
favorite playfriend of hers during church meetings or Sunday visits since his

mother had become the second Mrs. Victormaki the previous summer, just a few months after the first Mrs. Victormaki died, I had forgotten completely what I was supposed to be doing.

I had forgotten the iron.

Hurrying to obey Äiti, I whirled, too, and in the process seared the inside of my left elbow full flat against the burning hot flatiron, still held in my right hand.

Warm from the combination heat of flatirons and wood stove, I had rolled my sleeves up, carefully so as not to wrinkle them, so there was no buffer of clothing. Bare skin took the heat full force and melted.

Jerking back, I stared stupefied first at the iron and then at my arm. It didn't even hurt. Then I smelled the scorched flesh, and, like Mrs. Victormaki, I crumpled, too, in a heap of freshly ironed handkerchiefs, the iron hitting the floor with a thud, embossing the wood with a black design that Äiti never was able to scrub off, no matter how she tried.

In fact, I'm not sure that she wanted to. Its imprint served as a clear reminder of the transitory nature of peace and, equally importantly, of the forces that no amount of routine and order can control, forces of chance and happening that mold the days to their own pattern, willynilly.

Had Äiti ever allowed herself to use the word, I am sure that she would have described that moment as a moment from hell.

Had Lehti Aapo not suddenly appeared in the doorway, Suutari Erkki behind him, disaster might have tripled. But Suutari Erkki had come with his horse and sled-sleigh, hauling his sewing machine with the foot pedal, ready to make shoe packs should Isä and Äiti need a new year's supply.

Suutari Erkki, the shoemaker and felter, was infamous for the amount he could drink. I had once overheard Mr. Victormaki telling Isä that Suutari Erkki bought moonshine five gallons at a time from Harjun Kassu, the Lake Fourteen bootlegger. Äiti did not approve of him. But when he was sober, thin and emaciated from lack of food, he would come to stay with whatever family wanted shoes. Even Äiti had to admit that the shoe packs he made fit better and lasted longer than the ones she made. Wearing his homemade leather-laced boots with curved toes and singing while he worked, "Toodle-um-doodlum-doolum-dee," he went his rounds during the winter.

"Yenny, I'm a good man," he always said to Äiti when he knocked on the door to ask whether his services were needed.

The first time he came, she allowed him to sleep on a rigged-up bed in the sauna dressing room. Never again. He had brought with him not only his machine and leather and soaked wool but a generous supply of bedbugs, which happily infested the mattress and the blankets and the bedsprings. When he left, Äiti and Isä took the bedsprings outside, poured kerosene all over them, then burned them with a torch.

In Äiti's one-woman war against bedbugs, the advent of Suutari Erkki was usually eyed with dismay.

That Tuesday, he offered salvation.

Neighbors and friends often teased Äiti because she talked so fast, even faster than snowflakes flew on the breath of the north wind.

That day she outdid herself giving directions.

First, she told Lehti Aapo to lift Mrs. Victormaki and Verner onto the big bed; then he was to disengage Verner from his mother's limp arms and not to waste time gasping or swearing in Finn. He did as she directed—grabbed fresh linens from the table, undid one of the laces from his boot, and applied both onto some part of Verner. Then he wrapped the two into Äiti's good quilt and carried them, as ordered, toward Suutari Erkki's sleigh.

In the meantime, Suutari Erkki disconnected the sled with his sewing machine, tools, and materials from the sleigh, wrapped the warm flatirons in towels, grabbed the quilt from our bed and our outside clothes from their hooks beside the door, and lifted Maija-Liisa into the rear seat of the sleigh.

Äiti then addressed herself to me.

The sovereign remedy for burns was a smear of soft butter. But Äiti, appalled by the extent of the damage, opted instead to push snow into a pillow case, which she held to my arm as she motioned to Suuturi Erkki to help us, too, into the the sleigh, prodding him to move . . . move . . . move.

Then we were off.

At least, I think that was what happened. Concentrating on holding the pillowcase against my arm, I shook, and the world faded in and out and then disappeared entirely as Lehti Aapo and our home receded in the distance.

When I came back to myself, I was on Äiti's lap in the sleigh, wrapped in her shawl and bundled under Suutari Erkki's fur lap robe, regardless of the bedbugs. Maija-Liisa, her thumb in her mouth, had attached herself like a woodtick to Äiti's arm. My arm felt . . . strange . . . at once hot-hot-hot and yet terribly cold. I was sweating and shivering at the same time, and I wanted to cry, but the tears had burned away or frozen somewhere deep inside me.

Above the back of the seat ahead of us, I could see Mrs. Victormaki's tousled red hair, covered now with Lehti Aapo's plaid woolen hat. I could not see Verner.

"Is he alive?" I tried to ask. My teeth were chattering so hard that the words came out in staccato bursts.

But Äiti understood. "*Joo*," she nodded.

"*Mikä vaivaa?* What is wrong?" I tried again, harder. I liked Verner, and anyway thinking of him put my fears for myself on temporary hold.

"Don't worry," Äiti soothed. "He'll be fine. It is just his hand, not his whole body. When we get to Soudan, the doctor there will fix him just as he will mix something to make you feel much, much better. For now, don't worry. All is well."

Her voice, usually as soothing as the wind in the trees, cracked. I could feel her shivering, too. I could feel her fear.

All was obviously not well.

When the sleigh hit a rough spot in the narrow trail and my arm bumped, I tried not to scream. But Verner did. And off in the distance, but not so far in the distance, the wolves howled although it was day.

The bells on Suutari Erkki's sleigh reminded me of the fear I had felt before Santa's Christmas Eve visit, and we sped along the snow-covered icy path overhung with boughs of Norway and jackpine, heavily laden with snow.

Although the sun had peeked into our kitchen while I stood at the table ironing, it made little headway through the woven branches above us, and the snow beneath was blue rather than white or glistening silver.

The wolves howled again, closer. Did they smell the blood? Was it all Verner's blood? Was it *all* of his blood?

Äiti's voice shook, but she swallowed hard and asked, "Did you hear them? Did you hear the wolves?"

I burrowed as close as my arm would allow and nodded.

"Listen to the wind in the trees," she murmured.

I did. It soughed softly, an inarticulate *ooooohhhhh* all around us.

"I think Mummu Hölömöläinen is calling the wolves." Äiti's whole being stilled against me, and I could feel her thinking and remembering.

"The problem was the cold, you see," she continued. "And the number of windows. Of course, it was nice to have all of that sunshine flowing in through the ax slots without the girls having to carry it in burlap sacks."

The problem was the cold, I agreed, barely distracted. The Hölömöläiset seemed very far away, their problems hardly worth considering.

Äiti tried again. "It's even colder in Finland during the winter." Her breath brushed my cheek, and Maija-Liisa leaned closer. "And remember the Hölömöläiset hadn't had time to build a fireplace. They didn't own a stove."

"Or an iron," I thought bitterly.

She read my thoughts and hurried on, her soft words dancing accompaniment to the base drum of the wolves. "Anyway." There was a brief pause as she gathered herself together, thoughts and remembrance and voice melding against the cold and the fear and the pain. "After the first deep snow, which sent the bear and the wolves and the rabbits and the squirrels and the skunks hurrying to their dens to sleep, the cold fell in sheets of bleak, gray ice, shrouding the lake and the trees and the cabin in a frozen mist."

I shivered. Why on earth was she making us, cold already, even colder? Isä would have known better. If Isä had been there. . . . I stilled the thought.

Even Isä could not have prevented whatever had happened to Verner. And, I had to admit though it compounded the pain, which would have been better allayed with anger, the iron business was my own fault. How many times had Äiti warned me to be careful? How many times had she warned me that the iron could burn? She had praised me for being old enough to be responsible though many times I had committed the sin of pride because I *was* older than Maija-Liisa and able to do many things that she, younger, could not. This was not Äiti's fault, I knew, though I wanted to blame her and scream that it was and run away from the Monday washing and the Tuesday ironing and the Wednesday baking and the Thursday cleaning, run far away to Soudan to stay with Isä while he worked in the underground mines.

We were on our way to Soudan, I had dimly gathered, and I heard Verner's whimper and his mother's sob, and then I didn't hear anything for a while.

When I came to again, Äiti was shaking me, even though that made my arm hurt more, and telling me that I must not fall asleep. "Concentrate," she begged. "Concentrate on the Hölömöläiset. They were in trouble."

I tried.

$$\newcommand{\placeholder}{} \quad) \; \bigcirc \; \ast \; \bigcirc \; (\quad$$

Mummu Hölömöläinen was the first to realize how serious their situation was.

[*Of course. I knew that. It is always the woman's job to worry.*]

The children were so cold that they weren't even shivering anymore. Baby Vieno was turning blue, and the others were piled in a heap on the floor on top of Norway pine boughs with a pile of clothes on top of them. Even Father Jussi was silent. He did not have a plan.

Then Mummu realized it was all up to her. She realized that it was time for extreme action. And she realized that whatever happened, it could not be worse. So she took her *kantele* and went outside.

$$\quad) \; \bigcirc \; \ast \; \bigcirc \; (\quad$$

I sighed. Last Midsummer's Eve all of the neighbors had gathered at the Victormaki homestead, invited there to meet Mr. Victormaki's new wife and her young son Verner. The first Mrs. Victormaki had died the winter before, I knew, and her baby with her. In the cemetery on the hill, her grave had two markers, one granite block with her name on it and near it a circular stone pillow with an angel engraved upon it and the name of the baby girl who had died in her arms no matter what the neighbor women had done to try to keep it alive.

I had heard Äiti talking to Isä about it during the night when I was supposed to be asleep. I knew it was naughty, but I didn't tell them I was awake. "Too many babies in too short a time," Äiti had cried. "Just too many babies. Her body gave out."

I had counted the number of babies in the Victormaki household and only came up with one baby other than the dead one, so I didn't understand. All of the others were older—two younger than Maija-Liisa and another two between her age and mine and another four older than I. How could there be too many babies?

"And this one came too early. She should not have been lifting." I could hear Äiti crying softly and hear Isä's soft soothing murmurs. "He is a monster. I hate him," she had spat, murder in her voice.

I did not understand. How could she hate a baby? It made no sense.

"Do you know what we did? We wrapped the baby in wool batting and put it into the warming oven. Do you think that was wrong? But it seemed so cold, and it was so tiny and so blue. We didn't know what else to try," she sobbed.

Isä had said nothing, just "shhh, shhh, shhh," but he must have said the right thing because later she stopped crying and fell asleep.

Six months afterwards, on Midsummer's Eve, we went to meet the new Mrs. Victormaki and her son, whom Mr. Victormaki had brought from Soudan. She had seemed nice, and Verner had fit in right away.

Not like Tonttu Victormaki, Mr. Victormaki's oldest son, now Verner's stepbrother.

We were all afraid of Tonttu Victormaki. Once when we were at their house for a summer church meeting, he had told us to dig into the straw behind their barn for treasure his pa had left there for us. Treats, he said.

"Snakes!" we screamed, uncovering a writhing mass that slithered toward us, angry at being disturbed.

Äiti and Isä had taken us home right away. We had not gone there again until *Juhannus*, Midsummer's Eve. Isä had not wanted to go then, but Äiti had said that she felt sorry for some reason we didn't understand and that it was important that the new Mrs. Victormaki and her son know that there were friends around. So we went.

Maija-Liisa and I had not gone to play with the children in the barn. We had been happy to stay with the grown-ups, to sit on the birch logs drawn up in a big square around a bonfire and listen to them sing and talk. We had felt safe there.

The new Mrs. Victormaki and her son Verner seemed to feel that Äiti and Isä and the others were friends, and just before we all began the long process of taking our leave, she asked if we liked the music of the *kantele*. Then there was no question of leaving, for she went into the house and came out again with the stringed lute, and she sang. She sang and sang, sad songs of Finland. We listened and cried though we didn't know why.

I remembered the *kantele*, and it seemed right that Mummu Hölömöläinen, too, would have one.

Mummu went out into the snow [*Äiti continued*] and began to play and sing her own special song, one neither Father Jussi nor the children had ever heard. Mummu had not been born in Lapland. She was from Rovaniemi, and when she and Father Jussi were married and she came to live with him, she had brought along two things—her Rovaniemi costume of embroidered skirt and blouse and wesket and her *kantele*. But she had never played the *kantele*. It was her secret thing.

[*I understood. It was her secret thing, just as Äiti's trunk was her secret thing, not to be shared even with her husband and children. Everyone needed a secret thing, I knew. I always had one though what it was varied with the seasons. My favorite was still a creamy white rock shaped like a heart that I had found one summer day behind the sauna.*]

Mummu Hölömöläinen went outside into the snow and stood very still for a long while, and then she began to play and sing. Her song spun through the branches of the trees like wool on a spinner's wheel until it reached the ears of the rabbits and the bears and the wolves deep in their dens and awoke them.

"Ooh," they sighed. "We must get up. A voice is calling. We must go."

Soon the winter snow was spotted with tracks, some small with tiny pads and nails, some large and fat, some close together, some far apart, some neatly in lines, some hopping, some dragging a little, still sleepy.

Toward the Hölömöläiset home they came, one by one, the rabbits and the bears and the wolves and the foxes and the squirrels, lured and soothed by Mummu's song. Without fear, without anger, they moved until they came to Mummu, still singing in the snow.

And then the song formed itself into words, words about cold and shivering, words about what it meant to be human, to be lacking fur, to live in a den that allowed in the sunshine, yes, but also the cold, to be frightened, to be alone, to need warmth and kindness. . . .

And the animals understood her song, the rabbits and the bears and the wolves and the foxes and the squirrels, and they followed that song into the Hölömöläiset home, and they made it their den, made it warm with their breaths and their fur and their fat and their company, until the children were no longer shivering but instead were warmed, comforted.

Then Mummu Hölömöläinen set her *kantele* aside again, and she, too, lay down, her head on the neck of a brush wolf, its tail around her waist, and she too was warmed, and soon she too fell asleep."

"The wolf," I said, stunned, "it did not bite her or eat her?"

"No," Äiti insisted. "It kept her warm."

"Did it howl?" I wanted to set incredulity aside and believe. I wanted our wolves to be like those wolves. I wanted a fluffy tail around me, keeping me warm.

"Only when it was lonely or afraid."

"I feel like howling now," I admitted.

"I know," she said. Then she wrapped me tighter in Suutari Erkki's lap robe, and I sat up with surprise. It felt exactly like the tail of a brush wolf.

And then we saw the smoke rising from the houses of Soudan, and I knew that we too were safe and that the doctor would make us well.

I still have the scar on the inner skin of my elbow. It measures five inches in length, almost two in width.

Remnants remain of the other scar, too, the one that formed during the ensuing days, one all the more painful, perhaps, because for much of the next year or so it remained largely invisible.

Chapter 5

"Keskiviiko"
The Wednesday We Didn't Bake

D AY HAD SLIPPED INTO NIGHT before I came awake again, and even then I was loathe to reconnect with reality. My left arm lay next to me on a pillow, swathed in bandages. But I felt disassociated from it and from the pain.

By the time I had awakened, as Suutari Erkki carefully lifted me down from his sleigh, still wrapped in the brush wolf's fur of his lap robe, Verner and his mother Mrs. Victormaki had already disappeared into the immaculate white bowels of the hospital.

I had known it was Suutari Erkki, not Isä, because of his rank smell—a combination of Peerless chewing tobacco, sweat, and damp wool, overlaid by dried blood. He had driven the thirty-some miles in just his woolen pants and shirt, laprobes and quilts covering me and Äiti and Maija-Liisa in the back seat and Mrs. Victormaki and Verner in the front. But Suutari Erkki had not seemed cold. I think he had urged the horse on so forcefully it was almost as if he too had raced the miles away.

Dr. Hicks had given me something rich and sweet to drink when we first entered the hospital so I had been only subliminally aware of the burn on my arm being dressed and my body being washed clean of the bugs from the lap robe. I was still only vaguely aware of someone sitting on the wooden chair by the bed. Who it was didn't seem to matter as I faded in and out of a blessed velvet oblivion.

The glistening purity of white enamel walls and the bleached sheets and blanket covering me reflected the full moon, framed by the single window near the foot of the bed. As overcome with lassitude as I, the moon rose slowly, supported by the bleak, black branches of the leafless trees that lined the hills. Only when it lowered to rest beneath the dark horizon did I too sleep.

I awoke to an indigo dawn. Nothing seemed important to my arm, cocooned in white, or to my spirit, swathed deep within me. I did not want to

31

think of the last moment I really remembered from the day before, when the second Mrs. Victormaki had appeared in the doorway without boots or scarf, no matter the cold. I hid from the rigid sharp icicles of remembrance.

When matter hits absolute zero, it becomes immobile so all that moved was the blood dripping from Verner, whom she carried like a babe though he was Maija-Liisa's age.

He did not move. He just lay in her arms curled against her breast, gray-white as the shadowy snow, blood dripping from their jointure down an apron and skirt already dyed carnelian. Red.

When we had first met the second Mrs. Victormaki at the *Juhannus* midsummer fete, I could not find words to describe the color of her hair. It was red, but not red, not like the maple leaves in the fall or my winter mittens. Äiti later told me the right word. "Titian." I loved its rich, full sound as much as I loved the luxuriant curls that looped into themselves as they fell in waves and swirls, escaping hairpins and nets.

Her hair coiled around Verner. Red, but not the same red as his blood. She stood there until time, thawed by the heat from our wood stove because it was ironing day, moved on, and she and Verner fell.

Then everything reversed from stop to fast-fast-fast—Lehti Aapo yanking a lace free from his boot and retying it somewhere onto Verner; Suutari Erkki disconnecting his cutter from the sled full of sewing machine tools and carrying us onto the rear seats.

All the while I screamed, for I too had lost control and as I turned to help, I forgot to remember what I still held in my hand. The flat iron seered away my flesh as it imprinted itself on the inner joint of my elbow.

Normally Äiti considered herself a good healer, well-versed in the application of our Sodergren cabinet, and Kastren-Papa, noted for his skill in time of accident or illness, had just left two days before on his way to a nearby logging camp.

But she hadn't attempted a home cure that time. Instead Suutari Erkki had urged his horse in a headlong flight toward the hospital in Soudan. Soudan. Where Isä had gone just two days before to work in the underground mine. I had desperately wanted to follow him then. Now, I was there. But I couldn't muster up the energy to see if the silent form on the nearby chair was his.

I don't know how he knew I was awake. But his quiet voice entered the stillness around me and answered the questions that I was afraid to ask. "Verner is alive," he said. "I won't pretend he isn't very badly hurt. But he is alive. Dr. Hicks wants to keep you here, too, until he can be sure your arm won't infect. Äiti did all of the right things—keeping it cold and bringing you here. It will hurt for a while. But the nurse can give you medicine to dull the pain. Do you want some now?"

I nodded, not because of the pain but because I wanted to be far away from myself. I wanted to be back in Finland. I wanted to live with the Hölömöläiset. Nothing bad ever happened to them. Not really. Somehow, magically, the fish jumped into the wagon, the reindeer helped build the house, the door and the windows were made. Even the wild animals cooperated.

As if he had heard my thoughts, Isä mused, "But the Hölömöläiset had problems, too." Drawing his chair closer to the head of the bed, he reached out to stroke my hair.

"With what?" Sarcasm bit with more acerbity than would have been allowed under normal conditions.

"Pirates," he answered.

That caught my attention, and, for the first time since I had awakened, I looked at him, really looked. He was still wearing his mine clothes, stained a deep ocher. The hand that touched my hair felt and smelled unwashed, surprising for a man who had built the sauna before he built our house, who was never niggardly with wood or water, though he had to cut and split and pile the first and carry the second. I had never known him to forego a wash-up and a change of clothes after barn chores or his shift in the mine. He must have been worried about me, I thought, and some of the ice from around my heart and some of the anger I had nursed at his not being there when I needed him melted. "Pirates?"

"They came up river from the sea after freeze-up to fill out their crew," he explained. "As the men on their ships grow older, they have to shanghai new recruits. That's hard during the summer when the Sami people are following the reindeer herds. It's easier during the winter when they rest, doggy and tired in their winter dwellings. The pirates had had their eyes on the Hölömöläiset family for a long time . . . watching. Lots of children. Good pickings."

"Oh, my," I wondered aloud. "Would they steal the girls, too?"

"Rarely," Isä answered. "Only if they were very good cooks. Otherwise pirates are not romantically inclined. They like war."

"Ooh." Then I knew immediately who would be at risk: Eino, who had been tough enough to break through the log wall to make a door; Toivo and Sulo, the twins, who were slow, but big; Onnie, who could climb or fell the tallest tree; Matti and Urho, who were learning to use an ax; Pekka, Kalle, and Severi, who were small but good at making birch bark fish baskets and catching flies; surely Ahti, who could sing the waves to sleep. "Did they find the Hölömöläiset cabin?"

I thought they probably would, but questions helped move the action.

"They did. They surrounded the Hölömöläiset's log home in the middle of the night, hunkering down in a circle, their sharpened *puukkos* in hand, waiting for the boys to come out in the morning."

For awhile I lay quietly envisioning the scene, relaxing under the gentle strokes of Isä's hand on my forehead. He smoothed back and untangled the lank strands of hair that had escaped the plaits and ribbons sometime during our headlong flight from our homestead to Soudan.

"What did they look like?" I asked.

"The Hölömöläiset or the pirates?"

"Both." Yesterday morning a thousand years ago, the Hölömöläiset's appearance had been of major concern. "Well, neither." I could wait for details about clothing. I already knew that every one of the pirates had Mr. Victormaki's face. "What did they do when the boys came out?" They would have to come out sooner or later, and that would be the end.

"They didn't come out." Isä surprised me.

I didn't believe him. "They have to come out to go to the outhouse."

"Yes, but they didn't have to be the first to come out."

"Ohhh." I knew a lot of the Hölömöläiset stories by heart. In fact, I knew most of them so well that sometimes I whispered my own versions to Maila-Liisa as we lay in bed at night, supposedly asleep. But the last two or three stories had been new to me. I had not heard before about the animals being drawn by the music of the *kantele*. And I had never heard about the pirates. Whenever it was possible, however, Isä liked me to figure out parts of the stories myself. This time it was easy. If the boys didn't come out first, the animals did.

"Right." Isä smiled.

☽ ○ ✴ ○ ☾

THE HÖLÖMÖLÄISET HAD FOOD INSIDE, a lot of smoked fish, more than enough for breakfast. But they had nothing extra to feed the rabbits and the bears and the foxes and the squirrels and the others whose fur had kept them warm all night.

When the animals awoke, they were hungry. At first, the bears and the wolves eyed the Hölömöläiset speculatively. In the early morning light, Baby Vieno looked like a tasty mouthful, and Mummu was as rolypoly and toothsome as a haunch of fresh venison.

Fortunately, however, in the Hölömöläiset's sharing of their log cabin den, the animals had come to consider them litter pals, admittedly hairless and limited to two legs, but *sukulaiset* nonetheless, and thus inedible. But the pirates were another story. Although as lacking in fur as the Hölömöläiset, the pirates' cloth coverings were imbued with the tantalizing rankness of maggotty logs, redolent of crawling things.

The white puff at the ends of the red foxes' tails quivered; and the black-tipped crosses marking their backbones, shoulders, and legs prickled at the pirates' rabbity aroma, compounded of sweat and fear. In all, the pirates smelled like dinner should smell—a vague reeking emanation of fish and salty seas overlaid with grease and a hint of . . . pine needles? potato mash? juniper berries? . . . something fiery and potent.

When the pirates saw the black bears lumbering one by one through the reindeer skin covering of the door-shaped-like-Eino and when they watched the wolves slinking silently behind and around those thick, lumpy, claw-rooted stumps, the pirates did not stop to think. They ran.

It was a long, long run because the ship had been left far south where the river and sea had not yet frozen. Some of them virtually skimmed the surface of the ground and the water until, clambering up the netted rope ladders on the sides of the ship, they hoisted sail. Others—the fatter and the slower ones—were not so lucky. The harder they ran, the more delectable they smelled.

By the time the bears and the wolves and the foxes and all of the others returned, willing to keep the Hölömöläiset warm throughout the rest of the winter, they were burping pirate.

After that, whenever the animals caught a whiff of pirate-sea smell, they converged.

Only Ahti was sorry. He would have considered going to sea whether the pirates had forced him to or not. But Mummu Hölömöläinen said he was still too young to go off on his own, and the Hölömöläiset family stayed intact.

"Like ours," I thought gratefully. Then and only then did I reach out to hold Isä's hand and ask outright, "How is Verner? What happened to him? Will he be all right?"

For whereas the Hölömöläiset cabin had remained sacrosanct, the Victormaki homestead had almost been the death of Verner.

Although Isä's assurances, vague and oblique as they were, were meant to be reassuring, specific details were not forthcoming; and Äiti's lips proved to be shut tightly when I approached her.

I did, however, find out the truth of the matter with a tactic Maija-Liisa and I were always to use when kept in the dark.

I eavesdropped.

Chapter 6

"Torstai"

Thursday—A Sort of Housecleaning

V ERNER'S ROOM WAS RIGHT NEXT TO MINE in the hospital, and I soon learned that, if I remained quiet as a robin chick forming in its egg, I could hear not only sounds but words through the adjoining heat register.

Over a week had passed, and it was late the night before I was to be released to go home, the danger of infection having passed and my iron-burn mending. I no longer needed medicine to take away the pain or to help me sleep.

Verner had not been so lucky. I had heard him crying hard and asking for his mother, which seemed strange. I had overheard Äiti telling her she needed to go to the boarding house to get some rest, but she had refused to go.

Then I had not heard him at all. That last night, especially, no sound had disturbed the immaculate, white stillness.

I could not fall asleep. Äiti and Isä had finally acceded to my insistence that they go to the boarding house to bed themselves, and they had finally agreed that at this juncture Maija-Liisa needed them more than I.

Perhaps I was slept out. At any rate, I was sorely tempted to sneak out of bed and into Verner's room to see what was going on despite clear injunctions to stay put.

Then the hall door to Verner's room opened, and I heard Dr. Hicks' usual "Here-I-am-how-are-you?" But it sounded muted and a lot less cheery than usual. Chairs shifted, and I could almost see him leaning toward Mrs. Victormaki reassuringly patting her hand as he had Äiti's earlier.

"What happened, Mrs. Maki?" his deep low voice rumbled. "Neither the hand nor the child is healing. If either he . . . or you . . . would tell us, perhaps we could help . . . both of you. There is no one here but me," he continued, well-intentioned but bumbling. "I cannot help a great deal, however, unless I know the specific details of the accident."

There was a long pause.

Then the stillness shattered. Mrs. Victormaki's warm, vibrant voice was brittle as a frozen tree branch that could be whacked off with a measuring stick without the need of an ax. The words just fell.

"Tonttu. Tonttu Victormaki. Mr. Victor Maki's son. My . . . (pause) . . . stepson."

Even through the wall I could sense Dr. Hicks' blanketing empathy.

"He was in the woodshed," Mrs. Victormaki continued, "splitting wood. Verner had gone there to get a load of kindling to refill the woodbox. It was his morning job." The tone of her voice had risen as if in a question.

"Yes. I see." Dr. Hicks' voice fell around her like carded wool, thick and comfortable.

"No, you don't. You couldn't." Hers was shrill. I could not help but hear. "If I had even thought. . . . But it was too late."

"There was an accident." Dr. Hicks was clearly trying to help her along.

"No. No accident. I heard what happened because when Verner did not come back right away, I suddenly felt afraid, and I ran out toward the wood shed to get him, and I heard Tonttu taunting Verner: 'You little scaredy cat. You're too liver-bellied to dare . . .'" Her voice trailed off.

"To dare?" Dr. Hicks urged her on.

"I bet you don't dare put your fingers on the chopping block. I bet you're too much of a little city boy to put your fingers there when I have the ax in my hand. I bet you're not fast enough to pull them away. I bet you're too much of a city-sissy." Her voice mimicked Tonttu's voice exactly. "You don't think I can aim with the ax. You don't think I'm a good enough woodsman to hit the spot I'm aiming at. You don't trust me."

"'I do! I do!' Verner cried." Now it was his voice.

Then it was hers again: "He w-wanted so badly to have his step-brother like him. He wanted so badly to be accepted."

It was her voice, but not her voice. It had frozen again. "And me. I wanted Tonttu to accept me, too, not as a replacement for his mother but for myself."

"Yes." Dr. Hicks spoke quietly. "So," he pried at the ice: "Verner put his fingers on the chopping block, and Tonttu did use the ax, and he missed."

"No." I could barely hear her final words: "No. He didn't miss."

My heart froze as I realized what she meant.

Dr. Hicks' silence meant he too had finally understood. I heard the rustle of cloth as if he were drawing a shawl or a blanket over her shoulders.

She forced herself to continue, her voice shaking: "He hit exactly what he had aimed for."

After a long moment of silence, Dr. Hicks gently inserted the one final probe that was relevant and necessary: "Was it, the ax, clean?"

"No," she whimpered. "It was the broad ax, the *piilu*, the one that is only used for shaping logs. It was not either sharp or clean. It had lain on the ground since . . . last summer? It was caked. I saw it when I got to the woodshed and picked up Verner. It was . . . stuck to the woodblock and . . . stuck to . . . the . . . fingers. It was . . . rusty . . . not clean."

I gasped. Even I knew the risks. At the least . . . infection. At the worst . . . lockjaw.

They heard me. Clothing rustled. Footsteps tiptoed away. The hall door closed behind them, and I was left alone in the night, a thin wall away from the silence that was Verner, a little boy, just Maija-Liisa's age.

There was nothing I could do. Verner's life was not in my hands. Nor could he feel his mother's tender touch. His soul was flying even beyond the skill and power of Dr. Hicks' medicine. What could bring him back? Where could I go for help?

Then the answer came: "Go with God, my child," Reverend Lappala had told me when we left the final fall *kahvi kekkerit*, the church meeting, the last time I had seen him.

"And God is love," he always said.

I could not disobey Äiti and Isä and get out of bed, but I crawled to the foot of the bed near the window and looked out, wondering how to find God in all that wide world. I had not been to confirmation, so I didn't know any prayers except the one I said before I went to sleep. But I did know one hymn Äiti sang in good times and bad, whether she was happy or sad, because she said it gave her comfort:

Taivas on sininen ja valkoinen
The sky is blue and white
Ja tähtöisiä täynnä.
and full of stars.

The rest of the song was supposed to be *"Niin on nuori syndämmeni / Ajatuksia täynnä."* — "So is my young heart full of thoughts."

But Äiti never sang it that way. She and Isä were different, I recognized even at that young age, from the other grown-ups I knew. The other men never said "I love you" to their wives in public. I rather doubted that they ever did in private, either. The other parents didn't hug and kiss each other and their children as Äiti and Isä did each other and us. I had never heard the others say the words of love we heard every day. And, typically, Äiti had her own version of those last two lines:

"Niin on oma sydämmeni," she sang, "just like my own heart" . . .
. . . *"Rakkautta täynnä . . .* is full of love."

"Love" was not a forbidden word at our house.

"God," I prayed, "if you are love, please help to care for Verner."

I knelt and repeated those same words over and over again until a rose-pink blush touched the sky, the window, and my heart; next door I heard Verner call, softly, but in a relatively normal voice, "*Äiti, oletko sielä?*" — "Mother, are you there?"

My heart leaped with joy and hope, and I remembered one other part of our church's ritual. This one we always said in English: "From all that dwell below the skies, let faith and hope with love arise. Let beauty, truth, and good be sung through every land, by every tongue."

"But," I thought to myself, "*not* from *all*. There is one exception. Tonttu Victormaki. And," I added grimly, "we shall see about him."

Chapter 7

"Torstai"
Still

WHEN WE LEFT SOUDAN the following morning, the one left behind was not Isä, as I had expected, but Suutari Erkki, who had borrowed snowshoes and disappeared in the night up the Echo Trail toward the Paulson Mine.

Little did I know that it was not the mine that interested Suutari Erkki, however, but the accompanying entertainment, notably Meg Mathew's house, where he could find not only cheap bootleg booze shipped in from Canada on the P. D. railway but the enticing companionship of ladies of the night who wore marabou boas and satin shoes and not much else.

With those prospects in mind, Suutari Erkki had left his sleigh for us to use to go back to our homestead in Alango. Thus, it was Isä who held the reins and sat by Äiti in the front seat with Maija-Liisa and me in the back.

But unlike their usual companionable teasing and talking, Äiti and Isä were silent, the words they were not saying standing between them in wooden blocks. They rarely disagreed about anything, and normally, even when they did, dissension tended to twine into teasing laughter and conciliatory hugs.

Such was not the case on that long drive. Nor did they, who were always touching, reach out each to the other. Barricades had risen, and even Maija-Liisa and I felt locked out.

We knew that Isä had lost his job at the mine. The mine boss had ordered him back to work while I was sick, delirious daughter or no.

Isä had been overcome far more than I had ever intended by the guilt contingent upon having been far away when we needed him. I had been very angry with him when I awoke in the hospital, but my anger had ebbed in the wake of his concern.

His concern, however, had breach-birthed a formless living guilt: he regretted having left us alone on the farm. He would not leave me alone in the hospital, regardless of the mine boss's orders.

Thus, the money we needed to buy animals and seed for summer planting, the money that had been supposed to come from our sacrifice of Isä's presence, had been lost.

Money was the bone of contention, I sensed, but I could not believe that Äiti was angry because Isä was not returning to the mine. Some other factors were at work. No matter how I tried I could not figure out what they were.

The heaviness of their silence was lightened somewhat by the warmth of Lehti Aapo's greeting when we sped into the yard, bells jingling on the horse's harness. Lehti Aapo, noted for his reticence, was positively ebullient when he saw us, pumping Isä's hand and pounding him on the back, accepting a thank-you smile from Äiti and even hugs from Maija-Liisa without withdrawing. Me he lifted as gently as if I were newborn baby calf. When I clung to his neck and kissed my thanks for his stewardship of the house and barn and Dolly and for his swift action on that long-ago Tuesday week when I had branded my arm and when Verner had almost died, he actually rubbed his bristly cheek on mine. I felt a surreptitious brush of what felt a good deal like moustache-covered lips on my forehead.

Thursday was supposed to be cleaning day in Äiti's rigid pattern of days, but we did not need to clean up or in fact to do a thing: Lehti Aapo had scrubbed the house floor and the bedstead free of Verner's blood. He must have bleached the bedsheets because they were, if possible, even whiter than usual though, Äiti was to find out later, a bit threadbare. He had overdone the lye soaking. Only the imprint of the iron on the floor remained as a reminder of that day.

Thanks to Lehti Aapo, the sauna was hot, the barn stalls had been scoured clean. Dolly's rich manure had been added to the pile outside, and every pathway had been shoveled down to the ground. Lehti Aapo had been busy.

Äiti immediately set to peeling potatoes and onion for a *mojakka*, and a whole quart jar of canned whitefish was opened to complete the feast.

Isä took Maija-Liisa straight into the sauna, fed her a bowl of fish soup, and tucked her right into bed; but, ensconced into Äiti's rocking chair near the fire and quilted round, I was allowed to stay up to regale Lehti Aapo with the tale of my quick recovery and the hope of Verner's.

But I knew I served another purpose—as a buffer. Although Äiti and Isä were wonderfully kind to Lehti Aapo and to me, they did not speak to each other—not one word. And for the first time that I could remember in my whole life, they did not go to sleep together. I did not hear a good-night kiss or a whispered *"Rakastan sinua"* their usual final goodnight word of love.

It made my heart ache harder than my burned arm ever had and even harder than it had ached for Verner.

41

By the first time I awoke the next morning, heavy-hearted, Isä had already gone out. Instead of the usual humming accompaniment to Äiti's dressing, preparing of breakfast, bedmaking, rug-shaking, sweeping, and dusting, our happy house sat silent. Only the rocking chair creaked.

I did not want to get up.

Then the door opened. Isä burst in. Without brushing the snow from his jacket and mittens or stomping it off of his boots, he knelt by Äiti and held her; then they were both crying. I cried too with relief and cuddled close to Maija-Liisa's warm back and let myself drift away again.

When I awoke for the second time, it was to the sound of Isä playing his concertina, a *"kaksrivinen,"* and Äiti whirling in a circle of skirt before him, and all the tears were gone.

"Today is a holiday," Isä declared as we sat up in bed blinking and rubbing our eyes. "Today we will not work. Today we will sing and play and eat and tell stories. Today we will celebrate!"

And we did.

Instead of getting dressed right away, we danced in our nightgowns and shoepacks. Instead of sitting quietly to have our hair brushed and braided, we threaded our fingers through the tangled strands and let them hang in ripples down our backs.

Lehti Aapo had left after morning chores so our family had shrunk down to size. Isä refused to let Äiti do a thing, tucking her instead into her rocker and ordering her to tell us a story while he cut thick slices of frozen venison and fried them and potatoes and onions to a brown crispness in a cast-iron pan.

Maija-Liisa and I dunked *korppu* toasts into full cups of milk coffee into which we had stirred as many sugar lumps as we wished. Äiti didn't even say a word when we held the big double lumps between our teeth and loudly slurped great swallows of coffee-sugar candy.

"Did the Hölömöläiset children ever have a celebration as good as this one?" I dared ask, once it was clear that communication was running again in circles among us.

"Not for a long time," Äiti frowned, as if the Hölömöläiset holidays were of serious concern to her also. She had been cutting brown paper into paper dolls, and she paused, considering. "Not until . . . much later. In fact, near the end of winter, life became very hard again when they ran out of salt fish."

☽ ◯ ✳ ◯ ☾

ALL THAT WAS LEFT WAS CEREAL. But Mummu Hölömöläinen could not keep up with the task of making enough *puuroa* to feed her whole family.

[*Äiti's smile made it clear that all would be well for the Hölömöläiset, too, and we were not to worry.*] By the time Mummu finished the final breakfast bowl for Vieno, the littlest, the oldest boys were hungry for lunch. She made *puuroa* all day long and into the night, day after day, until she was exhausted. And the boys got very tired of hauling pails of water from the lake for her to mix with the meal.

Then Matti had an idea. Remember he was one of the middle boys, but almost as good with the ax as Eino.

"Mummu," he suggested, "stead a bringin' da water inside and makin' da *puuroa* here, why don' Onnie and me make a big hole in da ice and bring da meal dere? We c'n pour da meal into da water and mix up a big, big batch. It'd save you lots a work."

Mummu was delighted, and Father Jussi nodded proudly. His boys were getting as good at making a plan as he was.

So Matti cut a hole with his ax and jumped into the lake and took the bottom end of the cross-cut saw, and he and Onnie made a really big hole.

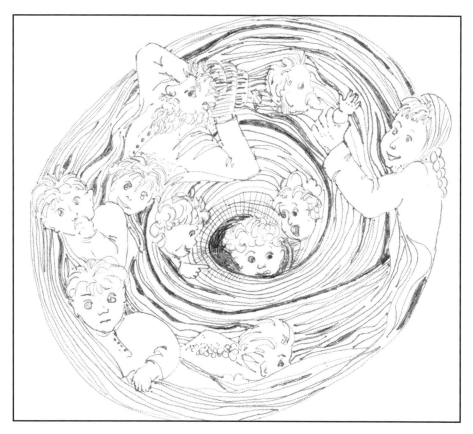

Then Mummu threw in a whole pailful of meal, and Matti offered to go back down into the lake to do the stirring. That way, he thought, he'd also get the first helping.

Mummu said, *"Joo,"* gratefully. Her arms were aching from days of stirring. Matti jumped in, wooden spoon in hand.

When he didn't come up and didn't come up, Eino got worried and then angry. "He be eatin' all dat *puuroa!*" he exclaimed. "I go down dere an' make sure he be leavin' some f'r da res' a us."

So he jumped in, bowl in hand.

When he didn't come up and didn't come up, Toivo and Sulo got worried and then angry. "Eino and Matti be eatin' all da *puuroa!*" they exclaimed, together as always. "We go down dere an' make sure dey be leavin' some f'r da res' a us!"

So they jumped in, bowls in hand.

When they didn't come up and didn't come up, Onnie and Urho and Severi and Pekka and Kalle followed suit. Although Ahti liked being on the water far more than in it, he jumped in, too. Then the girls dived in one by one until finally only Baby Vieno and Mummu and Father Jussi were left.

"No voi nyt piru," Father Jussi swore. "We not goin' ta get any brea'-fas' dis vay," and he grabbed Mummu's hand and she held Baby Vieno and they jumped in, too.

And that certainly seemed like the end of the Hölömöläiset.

☽ ○ ☀ ○ ☾

"Did they die?" I asked, wide-eyed.

"You'll never believe what they did." Äiti set down the paper dolls, her eyes sparkling.

Maija-Liisa and I leaned forward to hear.

"They came to America!" she sang triumphantly and jumped up and down and clapped.

We jumped up and down and clapped too, not just because of the Hölömöläiset but because it was such a happy day.

It was not until long after we ate Isä's special dinner that I thought to ask how. "How did the Hölömöläiset get to America?" I was drying the dishes that Isä had washed, and Äiti was cutting clothes out for the paper dolls.

"Oh, it was easy," she answered offhandedly, as if it really had been no problem at all. "They stole the pirates' ship."

"How do you know?" I scoffed. On a normal day I would never have dared use that tone of voice with Äiti, but on that golden afternoon all rules were suspended, and I had even forgotten about Tonttu and my plans for revenge.

"How do I know?" She sounded very smug in herself as she held up a dress to judge its height against a paper doll. "Remember what my name is?"

"It's Äiti!" Maija-Liisa exclaimed.

Äiti gave me a telling glance, and I answered slowly, "It's . . . Jenny."

"Yes," she nodded, "but my Finnish name is . . ." She looked expectantly at us.

I remembered. "Vieno!"

Maija-Liisa and I looked at each other in wonderment.

Anything seemed possible that day, and I looked forward to having Isä or Äiti continue the story and to having life return to normal.

But before I fell asleep, I had the nagging feeling that things were not, in fact, as blissful as they seemed.

The next morning I found out that my premonition had not been wrong. Things were not quite right, and it was highly probable that they never would be quite the same again.

Chapter 8

"Sunday on Saturday"

The NEXT MORNING THE PATTERN that had knit our days together continued its process of unraveling.

"If we're going to do it, let's do it right away," I heard Isä and Äiti agree over their morning coffee, and we had Sunday pancakes on Saturday. Again Maija-Liisa and I went braidless. Again the beds sat unmade, the floor unswept, the dishes undone, while we did the undo-able—we opened Äiti's trunk, emptying it of her secret treasures.

Green as the new growth on a balsam tree in spring, the canvas covered trunk with its wooden slats and iron bindings was substantial—about as tall as Maija-Liisa, almost three feet long and two feet wide, and bound by leather straps that clasped it tightly between the lock in the exact center and the clamps that clicked down on each side. The lid opened over a roomy upper tray thicker than Isä's hand.

In the tray, sugar starched to rigid crispness, lay the special *tuukis* we would use when Isä built our frame forever-house someday—crocheted filagrees of roses and pineapples for the tables, oblong antimacassars for the backs of over-stuffed chairs and sofas, a cutwork tablecloth with matching napkins for the dining room, and embroidered pillowcases and circular hot pads too fragile ever to be used except as decorations.

They were all so beautiful that even Maija-Liisa didn't try to touch them. She just stood, hands behind her back, saying, "Ooohhh, oohhhh."

My fingers ached for the soft hand-woven blue apron, which moved in ripples of cloth and braid. And underneath lay a white shawl so finely knitted that I knew it would pass the ultimate wedding ring test.

"I wrapped you in that shawl when you were christened," Äiti said, reaching out to hold me close. "You were such a beautiful baby."

For just a second, I thought I saw Isä's eyes look sad.

But then he turned his head back to the trunk, setting the tray aside, and uncovering the treasures neatly piled underneath. I vaguely remembered seeing the booties and caps, the sweaters and soakers, the bunting and blankets, the lawn christening dress with lace edging on the tiny collar and cuffs after Maija-Liisa was born. Piles of flannel diapers and sleepers, their pink ribbon ties carefully ironed, made up the next layer.

Äiti smiled a bit wistfully, I thought, as she unpacked and patted each piece.

Then we reached the heart of the trunk, and for the first time Äiti allowed us to see and touch her most special treasures, parts of her self that the trunk had kept inviolate. We had never seen her Finnish dress, although a few of our neighbors did don theirs at special times like *Juhannus*. As she took the pieces out and put them on, she gave them names.

First, she pulled on tight-fitting trousers or leggins, which were bound at her ankles with decorative red braids and tassels. Over them went the *skaller*, snow-white reindeer-hide over-boots that reached above her ankles with curled up toes but no heels. Hand-made thread of reindeer sinew held them together, and Äiti explained that they would be stuffed with sennan grass as insulation to keep out the cold and the moisture.

Her dress, a *koftes*, was dark-blue, always dark-blue, she said, with decorative braidwork of red and yellow and a lighter blue and cloth ribbons sewn to the sleeves and shoulders. After she cinched it with a silver belt, she stood up and whirled around. The hem stood out in a perfect circle four yards wide.

Silver brooches and gold rings, one for every finger, filled a fur bag. She slipped them on and put a bright red bonnet of fine blanket cloth, pointed in back, with long earflaps on her head.

Over the tunic-dress went a scarlet, blue and green woolen shawl.

But the three silk scarves in shades of magenta and emerald, red and orange—saved for special occasions—were even more beautiful.

Most of all I loved the reindeer fur *pesk* that was to be worn over the *koftes* when it was very cold. Loose, with full sleeves, it reached below her knee and cradled her in white fur.

"This is the way the women of Lapland look," she explained as we reached out to pet the soft fur.

My hand stilled. "Lapland women? Sami women?"

Her eyes twinkled. "Yes. This is exactly the way Mummu Hölömöläinen would look—and the girls, too—on their way to a wedding or a christening celebration."

"Oh, my." I looked her up and down all over again. Questions lay just behind the tip of my tongue, waiting importunately.

But Äiti was not to be pressed. Motioning me to silence, she removed the reindeer cape and the fur boots, the bonnet, and the dress; and motioning toward an ivory glove box, she settled down again in her white flannel night-gown. Isä lifted the box out of the trunk.

I wanted to ask about the Hölömöläiset. But when I looked at the box, which Isä held so carefully, I also wanted to shout, "Open it! Open it! Open it!" Something in her eyes held all of the words back. The earth shuddered to a stop, and our souls bumped into each other, jarred by the impact.

Seeking stability, I reached out for Isä; but he had moved to the wood stove and, opening the front door to the wood box, was jabbing at what looked to me like a pretty self-sufficient glowing mass.

Äiti ignored the cape and boots, the bonnet and dress that had so entranced me.

"Isä and I have not agreed about what to do with this," she explained, holding the thin, narrow box. "So we decided that we would leave the final determination to its owner." She looked straight at me. "To you."

I stood up so abruptly that I felt dizzy and almost fell into the trunk.

"Mine? It's mine?" The words came out like a frog's croak ending in a tree-toad squeal.

"Yes. Sit down here." She patted the floor beside her, waited until I complied, then motioned for me to lift the small carved metal latch.

When I did, the world lurched. Again I lost my equilibrium, forgetting even to breathe.

Unbelievably, even Maija-Liisa's tongue was cat-bit. For the first time since she learned to put one sound after another into a somewhat intelligible sequence, she did not say one word.

Inside of the ivory box, on the green satiny lining, lay stacks and stacks of coins. Monies.

I lifted one up to the light. It was a little bit heavier than the silver dollars in Isä's brown leather pouch but not quite as wide. Stars surrounded the side view of a beautiful lady with jewels on the crown that covered her hair and her ear. Thirteen stars. I counted them. Underneath the silhouette was the number 1861.

Äiti said she was "Lady Liberty."

On the other side of the coin, block letters for the UNITED STATES OF AMERICA curved around the top of a shield and an eagle; TWENTY D. semi-circled the bottom.

I was glad that Äiti and I had spent hours doing sums.

I took the golden sovereigns out one at a time and re-sorted them into piles on the floor, ten piles with five in each pile. Then I multiplied. The mul-tiplication took longer than the addition, but I finally managed.

In front of me on our rough planked pine floor, glinting in the firelight, sat fifty gold pieces, each one worth twenty dollars. The glove box had held one thousand dollars.

Äiti repeated her explanation. "They belong to you. Isä and I decided we would let you decide what we should do with them."

I sat back, stunned and discomfited.

Maija-Liisa reached down to disarrange the piles, but I did not chide her. To her they were playtoys, golden circles she could arrange into her own designs.

To me, they formed questions rather than designs. Why was this pirate treasure hidden in Äiti's trunk? Where had it come from? Why, if such richness were there for us, had Isä gone to work in the mine? Nothing in the pattern of our lives had ever indicated that such wealth existed at all, much less within easy grasp.

Could it possibly be true that it all belonged to me? I pondered the imponderable. That it had been a secret was clear. That the secret was to be revealed was clear. That there was a reason both for its existence and for its being a secret, I must ultimately know.

But did I really want to know? That was the sticking point.

Whatever it was, this totality had already created a rift between Äiti and Isä, albeit one that had seemingly been bridged.

But an unbridgeable chasm loomed before me. With almost every bit of my heart, I wanted it closed. I wanted the treasure returned to an unopened trunk, and the trunk locked, its secrets safely unrevealed.

I could not, however, niggle that dragonfly back into its cocoon. Curiosity too had hatched, and irrevocably, willynilly, it would fly, leaving its incubus torn and dry behind.

I did not even need to form the word. It shouted from my eyes. Why? Why the secret?

"The money is not ours. It does not really belong either to your Äiti or to me," Isä's voice resonated, despite the obvious effort he was expending to keep it calm, controlled, and gentle—normal. "It is not for us to use. It's yours. Your birth money. It is the golden key to your future, not to be . . . wasted . . . on present needs."

Äiti broke in impatiently, her voice fluttering toward him on dragon-fly's wings. "But her future is tomorrow as much as it is the time years and years from now when she has grown up."

Isä shook his head, but she persisted. I sensed she had said these words before. "Unless we survive the winter and succeed here, she will not have a future, at least not one worth experiencing. We have to buy seed. Livestock. It is our livelihood. It means our lives. Tomorrow and next winter are the future." Her voice rose impatiently when Isä turned away. Then it dropped.

"There. You see." She turned to me. "There it is."

I understood. What we should do with the money—that was the question; that, the chasm.

I almost laughed. How simple! I felt lightheaded with relief. If it were mine to use or give or save and if we needed it now, then the bridge was obviously already built. "Use it!" I did not hesitate for a second. "Use it," I repeated, firmly.

I understood Isä's reluctance to use what was mine. Always, both Isä and Äiti had emphasized to Maija-Liisa and to me our right to our own personal identities, to our private space where we could go to be alone, to our private parts that only we could wash, to our private dreams that no one else need know, to our own things. But no sense of personal claim tied me to the golden coins. They were not mine. Their symbol was the silhouette of Liberty. They should be freely used.

As I struggled to articulate those thoughts, to find the words to set them free from the cocoon within me, I was backhanded by a vicious reality.

Mr. Victormaki had hit Tonttu twice after the episode of the snakes—first across the left side of his face with the flat of his hand, then back across the right side with a resounding crack that jarred his teeth and neck, whatever it did to prompt his repentance.

Now the backhand struck me.

Why me?

I had never heard of "birth money." I surely would have remembered with envy if that had been a part of Maija-Liisa's inception. I had resented every other part of having to share Isä's and Äiti's attention, of hearing the exclamations of neighbors who came bearing small gifts of food or clothing when she was born.

Yet someone had given me money. A lot of money.

Who?

Why?

And there was another element to this, judging by Äiti's and Isä's continuing discomfiture. Something else was not right.

I sat back and waited.

The coins clinked against each other as Maija-Liisa played. A log in the *kakluuni* snapped as the fire broke into a small pocket of pitch.

"Remember when the Hölömöläiset disappeared into the hole the boys cut in the lake to make *puuroa*?" Isä asked.

I nodded uncomfortably. Had I known the word, I would have asked why the non-sequitur. The shift in subject was not reassuring.

"You wondered why they didn't come up and whether they had died there in the lake."

I nodded again without understanding the relationship of the Hölömöläiset problems to mine. The deflection of topic made me sick to my stomach.

THE CURRENT CAUGHT THEM. That was the problem. That was also the solution. The river that fed the lake was starting to move as rivers do in the late winter and very early spring, and it pulled them along as fast as the reindeer pulled their *pulkka* sled, bouncing them up high against the ice so they could breathe and then jouncing them down again. By the time it spewed them out where the ice had already melted on the Gulf of Finland, they were dizzy and shaken.

[*I could relate to that, I conceded and settled back into Isä's arms, letting him set me on his lap. The misadventures of the Hölömöläiset were always pleasant distractions, buffers instead of buffets. Curling into a ball as small as I could make myself, I cuddled close and shivered. Whatever the force, feeling one's life out of control was disheartening and disconcerting and distressing.*]

For a time the whole family lay on the shore, slowly recovering.

Then Father Jussi heard a noise. [*There was a significant pause so I knew it was important in the scheme of things.*] He shepherded his family into the alder brush that edged the shore and motioned them to scrunch down and be quiet.

It was a pirate ship.

Instead of being afraid, however, Father Jussi smiled, and his eyes sparkled. He had a plan.

Standing up tall and shaking off the water that was streaming from his reindeer cape, he strode toward the water's edge and hailed the ship, his voice assuming a tone and importance his family had never heard before.

[*We had always known Father Jussi's voice to be loud, but this time when Isä did the Jussi-voice, even the iron bedsteads bounced.*]

"Yo ho, pirates!" he boomed. Drawing himself to his full height, which was impressive, he continued, *"Minä on* . . . I be . . . Stallo, giant-king of da woods."

An echo from the nearby cliffs repeated the line twice.

"I vould match my strength 'gainst the pirate chief today. We see who be stronger, those who travel tundra 'r those who sail seas. We see who has the power." He spoke so slowly that each word, repeated, resounded, emphasized his challenge.

"Quiet, woodsman." The pirate chieftain's words rolled with the rhythm of the waves. Then he remembered that the pirate ship needed men at the oars, and his tone changed. The challenger might wield a mighty arm on their behalf. "Ah, woodsman," came a wheedling whine, "yes. Let us have a contest."

"Joo," agreed Father Jussi. "When I be the victor, I take your boat and rule sea as well as land."

"Ha," snorted the pirate chief, "I will be the victor. Then I will make you my galley slave, and you will rule only the sea, bending it to your oars."

"Se on puhuttu," said Father Jussi. "It be spoken, and so it will be. We see who be stronger. If you, I row da galley; if me, I get y'r boat. Agreed?"

"Agreed."

Then Father Jussi disappeared for a moment behind the rocks, returned, jumped into the sea, and buffeting the sea with lusty sinews, reached the pirate ship.

On shore, the remaining Hölömöläiset, Mummu and children, watched round-eyed as Father Jussi climbed over the gunnels and stood upon the deck holding high not one but two rocks as big as his haunch-sized fists.

The cliffs and the water redoubled his sonorous tones: "This rock be the earth. Water be its food. From the rock comes water but only if you be strong enough, pirate," he taunted, reaching out his left hand.

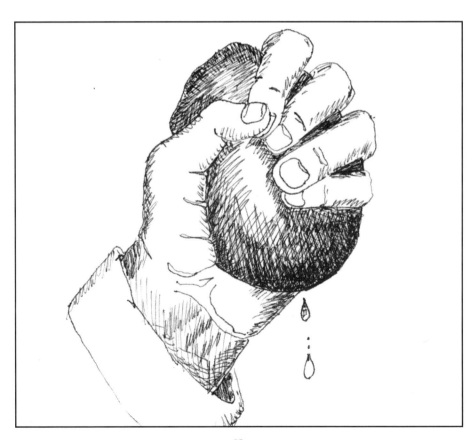

The pirate-chief took the rock in his own mammoth fist and squeezed and squeezed until the rock broke into pebbles and then into sand, but it would not release its water. "Never," said the pirate chief. "No one can take the water from the rock." Then he folded his arms across his chest and patted the hilt of the cutlass attached to his side like a third leg. "My sword and I say you be our slave."

"Wait!" Father Jussi held his right hand high to show another rock.

He sat on the ladder that led up to the quarterdeck, put the rock between his knees, and squeezed. He squeezed until the veins stood out on his temples like the corded ropes that led to the masts. He put the rock between his knees, and his hands pushed in on his knees, and they squeezed and they squeezed and they squeezed.

On shore, Mummu and the children squeezed tightly together to give him added strength.

The pirates formed a circle and laughed raucously, for the rock did not split into pebbles and sand. Then suddenly they stepped back astounded, for at the very center of the rock a small wet circle formed. And in minutes, to their total disbelief, from the very center of the rock, something spurted, and the rock released its water. Thus, the Hölömöläiset got their ship, and the pirates suffered their second defeat.

☽ ○ ✳ ○ ☾

"But not the pirates' final one?" I asked, drowsily.

"Not their final one," Isä admitted.

"But the Hölömöläiset did get a boat so they did come to America," I deduced. "And Baby Vieno came, too." I had not forgotten. "And when she grew up, she came to Minnesota and married you and had me," I continued, re-threading the pieces of my life. "And then I got the gold for a birth gift. It must have been part of the pirate treasure."

"*Sattuu.* Perhaps," Isä responded. "But not necessarily just that way."

"And rocks can yield water." If that could happen, anything could.

"Easily. If they are rounds of cheese that have been dipped in sand to look like rocks." He smiled.

Nothing is ever what it seems.

I had learned a lot in a very few hours.

Some of it I did not yet want to know.

"But there is an order, and there are patterns, order and patterns," Isä mused as we moved to the table to eat the salt fish Äiti had sliced and laid beside the *rieska.* Isä held it to my lips, and I did not even resent being fed as if I were a baby.

Order and patterns.

It was Saturday, but I did not want to go visiting. I did not want to go anywhere. I wanted to stay where I felt safe in my own house with my own Isä and Äiti and even my own sister in a pattern of days that came from Äiti's heart as the rag rugs did from her loom, to keep us warm and soften our steps.

But the gold . . . the gold . . . that was cold, and it still lay there on the floor. I did not care how it was spent. In fact, I was willing to give it away. Pirate treasure, if that was what it was, was always ill-gotten gain.

Why had it been given to me?

Chapter 9

"Sunnuntai"

Sunday

THE NEXT MORNING I AWOKE to the special stillness that was Sunday. It was, in truth, no quieter than the other days of the week, nor were they in fact any louder. But Sunday always surrounded me with peace.

On weekday mornings, Äiti and Isä had often dressed and had breakfast and made headway on their chores before they rousted us out of bed to get on with the day also.

But on Sunday, we all ate breakfast together, and it was always special—fresh bread slathered with butter and jam, slices of ham fried crisp and brown on the edges, eggs that smiled yellow eyes up at us or rose in golden hills in the middle of our plates. Sometimes Äiti fried mounds of thin pancakes, which were dredged in maple syrup. We talked about making syrup from our own maple trees, but, since we had not yet tapped our trees, Isä had traded for the syrup with our Chippewa neighbors who spent spring days, each family at its own sugar bush, gathering the sap and boiling it into maple sugar candy and, even better, into the syrup.

Sometimes if we had a surplus of butter and cream, or if the cream were starting to turn, Äiti made *pulla*, the sweet heavy cardamom biscuit that rose like bread from a yeasty-sponge. I was old enough to empty the black and brown cardamom seeds from their soft pods, to wrap them carefully in a corner of a flour sack, and to pound them to bits the size of no-see-ums using Isä's big hammer.

On weekdays, Äiti braided our hair so tightly we felt as if our eyes were pulling back, and in the summertime we wore simple cotton dresses without stockings or shoes.

But on Saturday night after sauna, she rolled our hair into rag curls, which dried overnight. She brushed them out on Sunday morning into ringlets that bounced when we walked, carefully, in stockings and button shoes, no matter the weather, a fresh handkerchief pinned to our blouses or to the tops of our dresses.

During the week, when the work of the day was over, Äiti's fingers never stopped flying over the small loom Isä had made for her or, knitting needles in hand, over the mittens or stockings that grew longer by the second.

But on Sunday, after we finished breakfast dishes and the usual chores, while Maija-Liisa and I dressed in our Sunday clothes and decorously set the table for dinner or waited for Isä to finish his work so we could attend church meetings, she did only fine handwork, tatting or embroidery.

"Church meeting" was a euphemism, of course, since our fledgling congregation did not have either a church or a full-time minister. But once a month, summer or winter, we gathered in a neighbor's home to celebrate our good fortune at being in this new land and to thank God for His blessings. Every family who attended these *"kahvi kekkerits"* brought a contribution to the dinner, eaten communally, for which the host family provided the *"kahvi,"* freshly ground and often cooked with eggshells for clarity, in honor of the day and the guests.

Äiti's specialty was either her famed angel food cake or *silli salaatti,* a combination of beets and pickled herring. The second Mrs. Victormaki had surprised everyone with new recipes she had brought with her from Soudan, specifically something she called a "rutabaga souffle," a concoction of vegetables, butter, eggs, and sugar beaten until it rose like a dandelion puffball.

But on the Sunday morning after those long weeks of chaos, I would cheerfully have foregone the curls, the shoes, the food, even the playtime we always enjoyed after the service while the grown-ups talked. All I wanted was a quiet day to weave my life back together.

Threads dangled loosely from the events of the last days, none integrated at all into the whole of my existence—my profound and heart-felt need to deal with Tonttu Victormaki; even more worrisome, the puzzle of the birth money's origin; the reason why Äiti had never worn the Finnish clothing; and underlying it all, the conundrum of the Hölömöläiset's having crossed the mysterious boundary between myth and reality with the divulgence of Äiti's possible identity as Baby Vieno.

It had seemed so puzzling after Saturday night sauna that I did not want another bedtime Hölömöläiset story or any story at all, for that matter. I had only wanted to sleep and awaken to find it had all been a dream.

But that was not to be.

Instead, a loud pounding on the door disturbed the Sunday morning peace even before I had a chance to savor it.

Äiti ran to open the door and gaped as I did to see Isä, his hands too full to lift the latch: one held his lever action 30/30 Winchester rifle; the other maintained a firm grip on the jacket collar of a squirming, wiggling, kicking, swearing child—a boy, who fell onto the floor in a shivering heap of dirty rags when Isä released him.

Tonttu Victormaki.

Isä had found him hiding in the barn, dirty, wet, cold, hungry, and irascibly importunate; he had not wished to be found, no matter his misery.

Thereafter, while my sister and I went through the motions of a normal Sunday morning, Isä dealt with Tonttu somewhere outside.

By dinnertime he considered the boy fit to join us, and the change that was visible was astounding. Sometime during the morning, Isä had cut the long, matted, manure-colored mop of hair, almost scalping him in the process. I later heard Äiti ask about that in a soft voice. Isä had just shrugged and lifted his eyebrows as if to say, "What else could I do?"

When Tonttu's hair grew back in, slowly to be sure, for it seemed to take him a long time to accomplish anything, it curled in wavy ringlets after sauna and on sweaty summer days. What I endured to make rag curls during the misery of Saturday night to accomplish the same effect, ah, that stoked the fire of my wrath.

At any rate, the Tonttu who (I wanted to say *which*) joined us at table was clean from the outside in, though rather precariously attired in cast-offs of Isä's that Äiti had not had time to alter—a pair of long underwear, arms and legs pushed up under a woolen shirt that had shrunk slightly from wash water a bit too hot. Pants had been a problem since Isä needed every one of his four pair—one for the barn, one for the house and summer work, one for the woods and winter, and one for Sunday.

Since Tonttu had spent most of the day shivering, sauna not withstanding, the woolen woods pants had been the obvious choice. Black, they had been made of wool so heavy they rivaled Suutari Erkki's shoe packs, thus offering more than adequate support when Tonttu stood but barely enabling him to sit. Sit he did, however, in the spot to which Isä had brought him, at the table with us just as if he had been a member of the family or a dinner guest.

I choked down fury. It was abominable to have to share our food and make dinner-time conversation with one who would have been more suitably fed in the barn.

As ladies, Äiti's lessons dictated, we were to sit at table with straight backs, whether we liked it or not, cutting our food into small bits and nibbling daintily, even when we were hungry. Ladies responded to questions with interest, listened to others, responded with civility, and offered appropriate comments with intelligence and grace, *especially*, Äiti warned us with vehement eyes, *when they didn't want to.*

It was clear from the beginning, on the other hand, that Tonttu had been taught no lessons in deportment. None at all. How and where he had eaten all of his life, I had no idea, but it definitely had not been at table. Instead of waiting for us to sit down, he had plopped himself onto the bench.

"Well," said Isä a bit too loudly when he had stood back and politely seated Äiti first, then me, then Maija-Liisa, "it seems as if we are to have a house guest for a while."

Maija-Liisa and I, having spent the morning in ignorance, sat straight.

I responded, as trained, "Good afternoon, Tonttu. Welcome to our home." The words were correct; the clenched teeth earned me a warning look from Äiti.

Tonttu reached over, grabbed an entire loaf of Äiti's fresh bread, tore off a chunk, and stuffed it into his mouth.

Maija-Liisa opened hers to comment. Isä closed it with the same hand that took hers as she took mine and I, Äiti's. Äiti reached for Tonttu's, but he had seen the butter plate and with his left hand was spreading globs onto the bread he held with his right.

Äiti closed her eyes. Isä cleared his throat. Maija-Liisa, taking that as a signal, began: "I am thankful for the food I eat. I am thankful for the world so sweet. For friends and family everywhere, for everything that I hold dear, I am thankful." The words were largely understandable. Äiti, Isä, and I looked at her approvingly.

Tonttu finished one chunk of bread, reached over and tore off another.

Since guests are always served first, Äiti asked politely, "Tonttu, would you like a pasty?" The savory semi-circles of light, crumbly pie crust held a mixture of rutabaga, onion, potatoes, and carrots, finely diced, and tender chunks of herb-seasoned venison. Äiti always made one for each of us and two for Isä.

Tonttu took three, stuffing a corner of one into a mouth already overfull. Butter oozed onto his chin, which he then rubbed with his arm and Isä's shirt sleeve.

Maija-Liisa and I had just had time to put our napkins neatly onto our laps and to say "*kiitos*" to Isä for serving us milk before we realized what had happened. Five pasties minus three. I did quick sums, but it did not take arithmetic skills for Maija-Liisa to see what had happened—Tonttu was eating our dinner.

Äiti offered the pasty plate neatly to Isä, which befitted his place at the head of our family. Casting a glance at our agonized faces, however, he waved it away. "I am just not very hungry this afternoon," he said.

I glared at Tonttu. Isä loved pasties. They were Äiti's most special Sunday dish.

As the plate went by Tonttu, moving toward Maija-Liisa and me, he grabbed a fourth and stuck it into the pockets of his pants.

Äiti sighed.

I thought about emptying the milk pitcher over Tonttu's head.

Maija-Liisa's face crumpled.

Quickly, Äiti slipped the last pasty onto Maija-Liisa's plate, cut it carefully into two equal pieces, and gave one to me.

The serving plate was empty. So was Äiti's.

Isä scowled. "Tonttu, I think we need to have a talk," he said, reaching a firm hand to direct Tonttu up and away from the table.

Tonttu cringed away from his hand, hunkering down in his place on the bench.

Äiti's straight back slumped, and another sigh escaped. Then she sat up, gave Isä her look, and asked firmly, "What will our Bible lesson be for today, my dear?" Isä always read us a chapter from the Bible on stay-at-home Sundays while we cleared the table. "The good Samaritan?" she continued, giving us all a speaking glance.

It was Isä's turn to sigh.

Maija-Liisa consumed her half of the pasty more swiftly than Äiti would have liked. But she was too busy exchanging eye signals with Isä to notice.

I considered the question. "How about a lesson on gluttony?"

Even Äiti choked.

Tonttu sat chewing as noisily and messily as Dolly in her stall.

I smiled. "How thoughtful of you, Tonttu, not to use your silverware. Maija-Liisa and I will have that much less to wash. And two fewer plates." I nodded at Äiti's and Isä's empty ones, and looked him straight in the eye.

Äiti opened her mouth, but I had said nothing that warranted comment.

I smiled again as Tonttu looked from his hands, dripping butter mixed with meat juice and pasty crust, to ours, neatly holding knives and forks. His eyes shifted like a weasel's to Äiti's and Isä's empty plates, and he knew he had eaten their dinner. He knew.

I knew he knew and smiled again: even a small victory was sweet. I had slipped the *puukko* in just far enough to hurt and slithered it out before Äiti could respond. Score one for Verner, I thought. The smile widened.

Thus did a new week and a new phase of our lives begin.

We were never to find out exactly what had brought Tonttu to us. Words were foreign to him. He much preferred action. It took Äiti and Isä most of that week to piece together part of the story, and even then they garnered only the husks of the truth. They never did thresh out the chaff.

When Mr. Victormaki had found out that his new wife had fled without completing the week's washing, ironing, cleaning, mending, cooking, and baking, he had been livid. The term is a good one. Calm, Mr. Victormaki's face looked sunburned. Angry, he blazed red all over, and the fire flew peripherally: he tended to scorch everything in sight.

The other children, used to being scapegoats, had scattered and hidden as Tonttu had tried to do. But when Tonttu had seen Mrs. Victormaki running with Verner across the field toward the woods and our land, he had headed in the opposite direction toward the house where, unbeknownst to him, Mr. Victormaki had come from the timber claim in search of a second pair of woolen socks and fresh liners for his choppers.

He was a worker was Mr. Victormaki, even Äiti admitted. It was not usual for him to pause mid-morning, no matter how cold the day. But coincidence, or fate, makes strange moves with its pawns, and that day he had returned in time to hear Verner's scream. By the time Mr. Victormaki had gotten to the door of the house, however, Verner and Mrs. Victormaki had already begun their headlong flight as had the children and Tonttu. Tonttu had run straight into his father's arms.

We all guessed what had ensued.

When Isä had taken Tonttu into the sauna, he had confirmed his own assumption: Tonttu's buttocks and back were shredded raw from a belting, the welts exactly the width of a razor strap.

But that was not the end of Tonttu's punishment; for, looking at a house bereft of food or heat, the fire having burned itself out before the anger did, Mr. Victormaki had acted in a way that was extreme even for him. He had pulled the sleigh out of the shed, hitched up the horses, thrown in some clothes and bedding and the children, and, lashing the horse to a frenzied gallop, had taken off for parts unknown.

"Good riddance," said Äiti when she heard.

He had no doubt surmised that the second Mrs. Victormaki would eventually divulge the truth not only about Tonttu's actions but about the entire way of life on the Victormaki homestead.

In later years, Tonttu was to talk about it sometimes. Once in a while he was even able to cry.

For when the sleigh and horses sped out of the yard, he had remained behind. He had been left lying where his father had felled him in the snow, numb from the cold, until he had realized that if he did not move soon, he would never move again. He had then followed Mrs. Victormaki's path, creeping across the potato field and through the woods and onto our land, finding refuge—some semblance of warmth, scraps of food, tastes of milk—enough to survive—in our barn.

But that morning Isä had gone there even earlier than was his wont since it was Sunday and he had wanted the chores out of the way. Hearing sounds, he had taken up his rifle and flushed his quarry.

Thus for a time Tonttu Victormaki took up residence in our house.

I rejoiced. In fact, I exulted in his coming, first because it was immediately evident even to or perhaps especially to his own eyes that he was abysmally ignorant of even the most basic rules of living. In fact, that which was evident to us must be equally evident to him. That he could have grown to so great an age, for he counted at least four years more than I, and yet have learned so little about civilized living was appalling.

It was, therefore, even simpler to expedite what I had set out to do forthwith—to make his life even more miserable than he had made Verner's.

Moreover, I took full advantage of the unwritten law against tattling to grown-ups no matter what the offense. Every night I went to sleep plotting the next day's machination, sure, too, that what Tonttu had done to Verner had put him so far beyond the pale that he would have been hard put to garner any sympathy even had he told.

When story time came that Sunday night, the only Hölömöläiset I wanted to meet were the ones in the old stories, the familiar ones. After all the events of those days, myth was far preferable to reality.

"Tonttu hasn't heard anything about the Hölömöläiset," I murmured, sleepy after sauna, hoping that Isä would take the hint and that we could go back to some of the earlier tales.

"So it seems it was summer," said Isä that night, "and the family roved out with the deer . . ."

His words took on a sing-song rhythm in which I found quietude; and I lay against his chest, listening not to the story but to the beating of his heart. For that while I was able to relax, not just into the world of Finnish folklore but into a circle that wrapped me in safety and love. It was a circle that Tonttu had never known; it was one that I was loathe to share.

Chapter 10

"Revenge!"

FOR THE DURATION, the last thing I thought of in the night and the first thing I thought of in the morning was the fall of Tonttu Victormaki. Eons later, when I read about the fall of the Third Reich, it was with a sense of being reborn. I had lived it all before. Unfortunately, to my dismay, my mind did not lend itself easily to Hitlerian plots and dastardly deeds; days slipped by without engendering a single nasty idea. I strove mightily to be mean and despaired at my ineptitute. Nonetheless, I thought, I would be watchful. When time finally offered an opportunity, I would be ready. And I was.

In the meantime, Isä and Äiti slowly assimilated Tonttu, gradually acclimating him to a civilized way of life if not, in his eyes, to a comfortable one. For Tonttu, it was culture shock. Äiti tried to gloss over his deficiencies, deftly and kindly teaching by example; but I relished every minute of his agonizing readjustment.

In the meantime, no one heard a word about Mr. Victormaki and the children. The fate of Verner, still in the Soudan hospital, remained in doubt, according to Suutari Erkki, who had eventually had enough of the dissolute life and returned to reclaim his sleigh and his occupation, making shoes and shoepacks again.

In March, the last of the winter's storms dumped three feet of snow on all of Alango, blocking trails, cutting off any kind of commerce, and virtually imprisoning us within the narrow confines of the house. The snow was so thick and heavy, the wind so strong, that day and night blurred together into shades of obsidian.

Isä ran a rope line to the barn so that he and Tonttu could take care of Dolly and find their way back. We did not even try to warm the sauna, and although Isä tried more than once to shovel open the door to the root cellar, the drifts defeated him, and we had to rely on the provisions that had been in the house when the skies fell late one Sunday night.

"Thank goodness we had a big dinner," Äiti exclaimed as we sat down to breakfast, kerosene lamp lighted on a morning black as midnight.

During the next five days, even her ingenuity was severely taxed as she reworked leftovers, concluding with a soup that grew thinner as the days ran on.

Keeping us all busy was Äiti's solution to the problems intrinsic to being in such close quarters, especially considering the looming pervasive presence of Tonttu. We therefore spent the days "in school" doing sums and practicing our letters.

I loved the idea of lessons—except sums—even though at that point they largely entailed learning colors and shapes, drawing pictures, and sounding out letters.

But Tonttu labored even with his own name and hated to draw or color or study anything by rote. Only at sums did he excel, although I was faster, only perhaps because I was more practiced.

Not until we had exhausted our brains and become cranky from the effort of thinking were we dismissed to our own devices. Maija-Liisa and I did well making clothes and houses for our paper dolls and inventing elaborate displays and performances to which we invited Äiti and Isä.

But Tonttu had no more skill at entertaining himself than he did at anything else. Finally, after watching him rattle around purposelessly, Isä filled the gaps in the afternoons and evenings in the way we liked best, with the tales of the Hölömöläiset. Since Tonttu had never heard any of them, even the old ones were new.

Slowly and gradually, especially during those long stormy days, Tonttu donned the garments of civility. He learned to wait his turn to be served at table. He learned to say "please" and "thank you," although the first sounded like a hiss and the second like a swear word. He accepted the inevitability of a daily wash-ups and clean clothing, and even—after multiple reminders—remembered to take his barn boots off instead of tracking slop all over the kitchen floor, though his pained expression made it clear that he considered that dictum a total waste of time.

After repetitive reminders about the virtue of being responsible, he appeared on time for meals and chores and learned to restrain certain bodily functions until he was outside or alone. He even succeeded in making Äiti and Isä believe that he appreciated all they had done for him.

But he did not fool me for one minute. I watched those ferret eyes shifting while he mouthed the right phrases like a trained jackdaw, and I kept my personal avowal intact: he would be taught to be sorry for his cruelty to Verner, and he would know the teacher to be me. Out of my enemy's weakness, I built my campaign.

Later in college when I read the first paragraph of Edgar Allan Poe's short story "The Cask of Amontillado," I immediately understood Montresor's specifications for the terms under which revenge could be satisfactorily achieved: "A wrong is unredressed when retribution overtakes the redresser." One must not only punish but "punish with impunity." In other words, I must not myself be caught. Moreover, Tonttu must be made aware of my acts of retribution. Only then, I believed, would Verner's pain be set to rest.

Like Montresor, I wanted to immure Tonttu behind the brick wall of a crypt within the catacombs. Since that opportunity refused to present itself, I was left with no alternatives other than those that lay within my power of invention, and at that I felt myself woefully wanting. Nevertheless, I persevered with my often fruitless plots until it was too late and I had gone too far.

When Tonttu graduated to going to the sauna alone instead of with Isä, when he could be trusted actually to bathe, I switched the gentler body soap with Äiti's powerful abrasive lye laundry soap. Before Tonttu differentiated between the sugar bowl and the salt cellar, I handed him the latter, which he typically dumped generously on his morning *puuroa*. I double-starched the collars of the shirts Äiti made for him and, when I could, used the sugar starch intended for *tuukis*, crocheted doilies. I savored the raw, red look of his chafed neck.

When at a Sunday *kahvi kekkerit* I saw head lice crawling in Suutari-Erkki's black hat, I carefully transferred as many as I could catch onto Tonttu's woolen *tussu lakki*, which Äiti had knitted him in shades of gray and red. His complaints during the ensuing kerosene shampoo gave me a sense of fiendish pleasure, for all the sounds of sympathy I made as he thrashed and yelped under the bite and smell of the vitriolic fluid.

When I mixed milk-coffee for the three of us or poured our milk, I made sure he got a full glass of whatever pitcher verged on souring.

When Äiti wasn't looking, I accelerated the process by slipping a tablespoon of vinegar into his glass first. Problematically, however, the food he had been used to when his own mother was alive must have been so bad that to this day I am not sure whether he ever noticed.

Buttons I sewed on his jacket fell off because I "forgot" to knot the thread.

Worst, or best of all, and I did feel guilty because it involved some discomfort for Dolly, when Tonttu was milking, I pinched Dolly or tickled her like a fly. Once she kicked Tonttu hard enough to make him limp for days. At the very least, her tail slathered his face and clothing with a noxious brown substance that smelled as bad as it looked.

In short, although these caused Tonttu only minor irritation, they mitigated my level of frustration as I strove to concoct a real plan.

For Äiti and Isä, who also spent much of the time during those next few months in despair, the turning point came with the story of the cloudberries.

I had heard it so many times that on the evening in May when talk about strawberry blossoms led to that favorite Hölömöläiset tale, I only half listened. Visions of smashed hornets' nests and swarms of attack bees surrounding Tonttu were mixed with a series of stratagems that arose only to be rejected: *if* I could find one of the hornets' gray paper cones on or near the ground, and *if* I could lure Tonttu into the vicinity and arrange for him to step on it, and *if* the hornets cooperated and saw him as the aggressor, and *if* I could get Maija-Liisa and Äiti and Isä and me well out of their range . . .

On the fringes of my mind floated Isä's story:

$$\mathbb{D} \quad \bigcirc \quad \ast \quad \bigcirc \quad \mathbb{C}$$

Wᴏ́ᴇɴ ᴛʜᴇ ᴄʟᴏᴜᴅʙᴇʀʀɪᴇs ᴡᴇʀᴇ ʀɪᴘᴇ, the whole Hölömöläiset family set out to do the picking, even Ahti, who was the baby then. But although all of the children loved the sweet treats and Mummu needed the berries to make jam and sauce for the winter, no one loved the treats as much as Severi.

Since the walnut-sized berries were scarce that year, Father Jussi made a plan: "When you bick," he told the children, "use first y'r left hand and then y'r right. Berries dat go in y'r left hand, you c'n eat. But da ones that you bick wit y'r right hand go into Mummu's baskets for all a' us. 'Member," his voice rumbled storm warnings, "left you eat; right you share."

Mummu set the girls to making baskets out of birch bark, one for each picker. Eino and Matti used their *puukkos* and axes to loosen and split the bark, and the twins scouted for the best patches.

Father Jussi hung the *kamse,* the birchbark cradle in which baby Ahti slept, from a sturdy branch so the wind could rock him to sleep. Perhaps that was the reason why all of his life Ahti was to dream of sailing onto a swaying sea in the wake of the wind.

Onnie rigged up a kind of travois out of the trunks of two young trees so that the reindeer could be hitched up to poles, one on each side, joined in the back, and thus carry home our baskets of berries.

Then the picking began, and each one remembered Father Jussi's directions—left hand for the picker; right hand for the family. Every one, that is, except Severi, who loved the cloudberries more than anything.

When no one else was near the baskets, he sneaked there, pretending to empty his berries in with the rest. In reality, every time he approached the baskets, his birch bark container was empty. He did not use it to drop berries in. He used it to scoop berries out. He went to the basket so often that Father

Jussi and Mummu praised him for being the fastest picker of all. It did not occur to them to wonder why, although everyone was picking hard and fast, the level of berries in the baskets was remaining much the same.

"Did he eat them all?" asked Maija-Liisa, wide-eyed. At least that was what it sounded like. Sometimes her meaning came from context.

"As many as he could, and that was a lot," answered Isä.

"Did he get sick?" Maija-Liisa often had been reminded of her own previous summer's overindulgence in blueberries.

"Of course he did," I broke in, impatiently. We had heard Isä preach this lesson before, carefully masked by the Hölömöläiset, of course, every time we were selfish. "Of course he got sick and threw up, and of course everyone knew what he had been doing when they saw the raspberry cud."

"Were Mummu and Father Jussi mad?" Tonttu threw in the question, caught by the story in spite of himself. "Did he get a licking?"

I gave him a contemptuous glance. What kind of parents did he think the Hölömöläiset were?

"No," Isä remarked offhandedly. "Mummu and Father Jussi had a better punishment up their sleeves." He paused, waiting for us to ask.

We did. "What?"

"They stopped the sun from setting and told Severi that they would not allow night to come or him to sleep until he and he alone refilled the baskets."

"They couldn't do that! No one can stop the sun!" Tonttu's contempt surpassed mine. "The sun always rises, and the sun always sets, doesn't it, Äiti?" Tonttu appealed to the only one of us he truly trusted.

Äiti looked uncomfortable and bit her lower lip. "Not in Finland. Not in the summer," she admitted a bit regretfully. Tonttu had for once been certain that he was right. Since he had come to live with us, it had to have felt to him as if he were wrong about everything, which in fact he was.

"That isn't fair!" he shouted, jumping up from the floor to stride back and forth across the small room whose confines had often that winter imprisoned him in rules. There was always, it seemed, a right way and a wrong way to do everything; and his way was never right. "All he did was eat a few berries!"

"But," Isä's voice, though quiet, was firm, "he selfishly put what was good for him before what was good for the family."

"What if what was good for the others was never good for him?" Tonttu cried. "What if he didn't feel like a part of the family? What if he was always treated like an outsider?"

The four of us sat back in amazement. Heretofore Tonttu's conversational ploys had been largely monosyllabic: *"joo" eli "ei,"* yes or *no* and not much else. Now, standing alone by the table and pounding on it with his fist, he verbalized full sentences, and the words blew out like a dragon's breath, noxious and full of fire. "Why should Severi care about the others when they didn't care about him? Eino and Matti had their axes and *puukkos,* and the twins had each other, and the girls all stuck together, and everybody took care of the babies, but he was alone! Alone! So what if he took a few berries! It wasn't fair for them to punish him all the time! It wasn't fair!"

Then he ran out the door, and the walls shook as he slammed it behind him. The air around us resonated with his anger.

Isä started to get up to go after him, but Äiti motioned him back. "He knows we are here," she said softly. "Let him come to us when he is ready."

But she carried the kerosene lamp to the window and balanced it carefully on the sill where Tonttu could see it from outside. Then we heard the clung and thud of the ax in the woodshed and the sharp clang as the sledge hammer hit the splitting maul. We slept fitfully all that night and awoke to that same rhythm.

The next morning Tonttu came to the breakfast table, his eyes swollen and his face gray, his hands molded into ax-handle claws.

But he went to the window and took the lamp down and carried it to the table. "Like the sun, it will not go out until the punishment is over," he said.

The words lurched out, hesitantly, as a wagon would move through deep ruts. Then he looked at Äiti, and, without shifting his gaze, he held the lamp up where she could reach it.

Understanding, although we did not, she blew out the yellow flame.

And then, so softly I wasn't sure that I had heard him, he breathed, *"Kiitos"*—"Thank you" and collapsed, sleeping most of that day and all of the following night.

The next morning, just as if a full thirty-six or more hours had not intervened, Tonttu paused as he poured thick, rich *kerma,* cream, on his *puuroa* to comment, "Mummu and Father Jussi didn't really stop the sun."

"No," Isä admitted, "it happens naturally. In that part of Finland at the height of the summer, the sun does not set. But Severi believed they could stop the sun, and that was all that was important."

Tonttu looked at him steadily as Isä continued, "Where *lapsi*—a child—is concerned, parents seem to—and often do—hold that much power." Isä poured his coffee into the saucer and took a considered sip before he went on. "What the children do not often realize is that parents are only human and make mistakes, too. Sometimes bad ones. Mummu and Father Jussi did not really make him fill all of those baskets. That would have been impossible. And they did not hold back the sun."

Tonttu digested that along with his *puuroa.* I noticed for the first time that his manners had become almost as good as Isä's. His napkin lay on his lap. His knife and fork were held in the correct hands. He had sprinkled one teaspoon of sugar on his cereal and had only taken two slices of *pulla.* Instead of gobbling his food, he was eating . . . oh, still rapidly, but at a polite pace, finishing just a bit before the rest of us. And he waited to say *kiitos* to Äiti before he got up.

As Isä did every morning, Tonttu took to going into the sauna first thing before breakfast to wash his face and sauna-sluice his hair, which he then combed flat to his head although it was too curly to stay that way for long. And increasingly, no residual stains or crumbs left evidence of the previous day's meals on his shirt or pants.

He had come a long way.

The ensuing days were to show how far.

One thing he had learned from his father was how to work. He had never, even I had to admit, been derelict in his duty. But during the days that followed he outdid himself. Thanks to the long night of splitting not only the chunks of poplar from our woodlot but the residue of years of pain, he had filled the woodshed.

By late spring after breakfast and morning barn chores, he began on the garden, plucking every weed out by the roots, thinning the rows of baby carrots as soon as they were ready, hilling the young potato plants, picking worms off every single small round cabbage, hoeing and working every inch of soil.

By early summer, even Äiti could not find one fault with the look of the garden: meticulous, even rows of green sprouted above freshly watered dark, rich, well-tilled soil. It was a masterpiece.

In addition, he began to scythe the long grass and hay from around the house to keep the woodticks at bay. In the process, he uncovered some clumps of wild flowers that he carefully preserved and replanted right alongside the house—not only the ordinary ox-eye daisies, but some feathery yarrow and delicate pink shooting star, pasture rose, thimble berry, and butterfly weed. From the marshy area by the artesian well, he picked vasefuls of blueflag for the table, presenting them to Äiti as if they were hothouse roses.

With every thump of the ax or stroke of the hoe, with every swish of the scythe, I hated him more. Around his head swam, in my eyes, not the halo Äiti and Isä were increasingly envisioning, but a shifting foglike miasma of pictures—Verner, drenched in his own blood. Me, my elbow burned almost to the bone.

When, one Sunday, Isä read aloud the "Prodigal Son," every word caked blood around my heart. There had been no revenge. I had failed.

And on Mothers' Day when our small congregation met under the Norway pines on the hill where the church would one day rise, log by log, Äiti and Isä said to everyone who arrived and sat on the square of birch logs around the bonfire, "You remember Tonttu, our fosterling?"

He had even been absolved of the curse of being a Victormaki.

The bouquet of trailing arbutus he brought Äiti was bigger than mine, and I wanted to stomp it into the ground. I was approaching the limit of my endurance one night in June as, reciting the litany of the Hölömöläiset boys, we got to Severi. Tonttu held up his hand to stop us at the final line and proffered his own version. "And Severi, last of those Finns" became "Severi, sad for his sins."

Äiti shook her head and hugged him hard. Isä hugged him, too.

I nearly threw up.

Tonttu knew how I felt, of course. I was sure he gloated in it. It had been, in words I later learned, "game, set, and match," with him the winner. If life were cribbage, I had been skunked, and he had scored a perfect twenty-nine. Baseball? I'd been shut out. He had taken the hat trick, and, underneath the mask I wore to hide my feelings from Isä and Äiti, I seethed with the fury of a pit of rattlesnakes or a nest of vipers, disturbed. I protected my anger with the fury of a mother bear whose nursing cub is in jeopardy. I hated him with a passion, a hatred that for a time far outweighed any other of my concerns.

Chapter 11

"Heinäkuu"

July

Fort-Chu-lie—Independence Day—dawned hot and still. Coffee, cardamom *pulla* with butter, and bowls of sweet wild strawberries made a sketchy breakfast eaten on the run instead of at table as we hurried to get ready to go to the Finlander Beach at Lake Leander, ten miles or so away.

Äiti, Maija-Liisa, and I wore dresses of cool white lawn. Without argument Isä and Tonttu donned long-sleeved shirts, knotted their ties, and shrugged their shoulders into woolen suit coats, Tonttu's cut down from a jacket donated by Suutari Erkki and worn by him in earlier days on excursions to Elysian Fields. Äiti had laid them out, starched and ironed and brushed, and her flashing eyes had brooked no discussion although Tonttu had tried to demur.

Isä had milked Dolly and let her out to forage at will until we returned. By the time Äiti had brushed our curls around her finger, King was hitched to the wagon. Isä had lifted straw bales onto the flat bed on which Maija-Liisa, Tonttu, and I could sit and covered them with a blanket so our good clothes would stay neat.

Äiti had tied her special angel food cake and two loaves of fresh *rieska* into square dish cloth carriers to protect them from flies. From the root cellar, Isä had taken a pailful of last summer's potatoes and the last of the onions and carrots and rutabaga, somewhat shriveled but adequate for the *kala mojakka*, fish stew, that would boil in communal pots all afternoon. Although the men hoped to supply fresh-caught northerns and crappies for the fish stew, we also took two jars of canned whitefish just in case.

By evening we were always ravenous when fresh wood was added to the fire and the fish thrown into the pot hanging above it from a metal tripod there to boil until the scum slithered over the edges. Then, fresh butter and cream were added, and we ladled the salty, savory richness into our bowls.

Black peppercorn and allspice nuggets floated on the thick ivory-gold sea into which we dipped boats of fresh *rieska,* thick with butter, washed down with buttermilk, kept cold in two-quart Mason jars that had been lowered into the lake.

In Finland at this season the sun doesn't set at all. In Alango it does, but we had time to sing and dance and savor the long evening before we headed home in the cool mist of twilight, long, long after bedtime, exhausted not only from eating and dancing but from running about and swimming and playing keep-away and screaming as the boys pushed the girls into the lake and the girls splashed the boys in return and the little ones were warned not to go into the lake at all because of the dropoff: "One minute it is shallow and sandy, and the next minute the bottom drops off into a black darkness that goes down and down and down all the way to nowhere."

The little ones paddled their feet in anyway, and the mothers worried and talked and laughed, and the fathers fished and talked and gradually shed their coats and ties and rolled up their sleeves and played horseshoe and sneaked to the top of the hill for a taste of *kalja,* rich brown beer, or sometimes even some moonshine.

The only part of the day we did not enjoy was the jouncing, bouncing ride west on the two gravel ruts euphemistically called Highway 22, up the Tupun Kallio hills where the blueberries grew, past Nukala's small corner store, closed for the day because they, too, were on their way to the lake, past Hagglund's swamp, breeding ground for feisty mosquitoes, past Hagglund's barn and house, where Harry Hagglund brought the mail from the train depot in Angora, to be picked up as convenient, then left, south, on Highway 25, also little more than a barely passable wagon trail through the woods.

The woods were, however, pockmarked by small farmsteads along the way—Laine's and Leinonen's, Korte's by the first swampy spot, well-corduroyed with swamp spruce—and by cleared spots, where a hall was to be built at the corner of the Goodell Road and the North Star School would open for children in the Buhl District in the fall, and then up-up-up Ticklebelly Hill until our bellies did tickle like a rollercoaster ride.

Except for the creaks of the jouncing, bouncing wagon and the bells on King's harness, the ride was quiet. I concentrated on holding onto the side of the wagon, trying not to wrinkle my dress. Tonttu leaned forward, his right forefinger inside of his collar, holding it as far away from his raw, red neck as he could. I had been successful with sugar-starching again. He watched Isä's skillful driving with total concentration and abject envy.

King required skillful driving. Still young, he tended to be skittish.

Of all of the purchases Isä had made with my birth money, King was the most significant. Standing at least seventeen hands high, he had character and charisma and a mind of his own; yet once Isä had seen him, he could brook no other animal. It was true that King was not and never would be truly a farm horse. Hitching him to a plow was a travesty.

Yet in light of Isä's and our obvious and total adoration, King condescended to accept even the most demeaning jobs as needful in the great scheme of things, necessary evils as it were, and the resultant treats, praise, and currying made them palatable if not pleasant.

It was clear again that morning, however, that as a carriage horse he had found his destiny, even if the carriage was only a farm wagon, largely homemade. Head erect, mane flying, hoofs prancing, tail aloft like a banner, he executed the dubious route with panache.

Tonttu dreamed of driving him . . . or riding him . . . and was thus in another world. Only Maija-Liisa truly suffered. She never was to handle traveling with ease, being prone to motion sickness. By the time we reached the school section, she was as white as her dress. By the time we reached the creek by Korven Kyla, she had turned green. And when the rest of us squealed as we bumped over Ticklebelly Hill, she threw up her breakfast all over her dress. Had I been thinking clearly, I would have realized this inevitability, and I cursed myself for not having moved her closer to Tonttu.

But I too had been lost in a daydream, as I so often was during those days after we opened the trunk, thinking of ways I could spend my birth money, mulling over the relative merits of the dresses pictured in the new Sears and Roebuck catalog. Eventually Äiti would allow Maija-Liisa and me to cut paper dolls of the stylish people in their elegant clothes. But until we had all shopped our fill, the book was sacrosanct.

I knew that Äiti coveted the handsome black walnut parlor clock with its six-inch dial, bronze ornaments, and plate glass mirrors. I knew Isä yearned for an extension top cabriolet with front and rear seats upholstered in green velvet, a buggy elegant enough even for King. I had seen Tonttu studying the Stop Thief Trap for rabbits, minks, and skunks, no doubt planning to make enough money to buy a bicycle. And Maija-Liisa had opened the book to the dolls on page 914 so often it fell there of its own accord.

I could not help feeling a bit smug about the golden coins in the glove box in the trunk that were all mine except for those that had been spent on necessities for survival. Those pieces of pirate treasure did not belong to Tonttu. They did not belong to Maija-Liisa. They were not, under normal circumstances, even to be used by Äiti or Isä. They were mine. The circumstances under which they had been generated were a mystery, it was true. At times that did cause a qualm. But the fact of their being was indisputable, eminently satisfying. I needed them during those days.

Tonttu had continued to insinuate his way into our family, to ingratiate himself to Äiti and Isä, to set my teeth on edge as he set himself up to be an exemplary young man and, to my infinite dismay, largely succeeded.

No word had come back to anyone in the community about his father and the other children, where they had gone or what they were doing. No one returning from Soudan had any definitive answer to questions about Verner either.

In the meantime, as Tonttu waited, suspended from his normal reality, there seemed to be no limit to his willingness to fetch and carry for Äiti, to find jobs to do for Isä, to be neat and polite and responsible, an infuriatingly model gentle man. It made me sick not just to have to watch him in action but to realize that neither Äiti nor Isä saw through his mask. I, on the other hand, was sure that behind the civilized facade he had adopted still lurked the soul of a snake.

Between us lay a no man's land wherein in public we observed the rules of correct conduct. Otherwise, I could just manage to coexist if he could just manage to leave me alone. In the meantime, I nursed my wrath, ignoring the niggling sense of unease that it was not Tonttu who was now in the wrong; it was I.

For months the momentum of my life had been controlled by the need to make Tonttu Victormaki pay for his cruelty to Verner. I had learned the lessons of revenge too well and begun to feed on them, like the bloodsuckers that lurked beneath the dead logs on the shore of Lake Leander.

When Isä realized the Maija-Liisa had lost her breakfast, he set the brake on the wagon and lifted Äiti down. She made murmurous soothing sounds and cleaned the child up. She was a mess.

But the creek we had just traversed was high enough so that Isä could rinse off her clothes. Laid over the wooden bridge railing in the hot morning sun, her bloomers and shirt, slip, dress, and stockings would dry very soon. In the meantime she meandered happily toward the ox-eye daisies growing along the roadside.

We had stopped in the cool shade under a tall, thick stand of Norway pine. Isä and I settled back on the carpet of red pine needles.

"Actually," Isä mused, "it is good to stop hurrying. Don't go too far, or Stallo will catch you!" he called jokingly after Maija-Liisa.

"Who is Stallo?" Tonttu asked, lowering himself down by Isä and unbuttoning his collar.

"You've never heard of Stallo?" Isä's question was somewhat rhetorical: Tonttu had never heard of anything.

"He was a giant, of course," I threw in impatiently. "A mean giant, mean as the pirates, and he lived in a hut in the forest with his wife, and they ate children."

Tonttu cast me an acrimonious glance.

He made me sick.

Isä did not see me feign a retch. His eyes were closed. A light breeze rustled the boughs far above us. The pine needles smelled so good that I set about gathering enough to make a sachet for my clothing drawer. Äiti wove daisies into bracelets and tiaras.

Tonttu sat very still.

"It all began soon after the Hölömöläiset took over the pirate ship," Isä began.

$$\text{☽ ○ ❋ ○ ☾}$$

WHILE FATHER JUSSI WAS RESTING from the effort of outwitting the pirate chief, and Mummu was scrubbing and scouring the decks and cabins clean of pirate smell, the boys were sent to gather the reindeer and herd them toward the ship; the girls, to pick enough sennan grass to line everyone's boots and the baby's cradle or *kamse* for as long as their voyage to Amerika would last.

It was a long walk back over the tundra to the cabin they had left behind when they jumped into the lake to eat *puuroa* and were caught by the spring currents and carried to the sea. Like all Lapland children of the Sami people, they had an infallible sense of direction. But the long trek tired them out. Moreover, the first smudges of spring insects had metamorphosed into clouds of black.

Finally Eino the oldest could stand the bugs no longer. He told the others to hunker down around a flat rocky spot while he built a smoke screen.

[*I shivered as I thought about mosquitoes. In early June after a soggy wet two weeks of May rain, the swarms had laid siege to our house and yard. Äiti had rigged up cheesecloth nets to cover our heads as we hung clothes and worked outside. But I had once counted ten mosquitoes feeding on the hand holding a clothespin, and Isä held the record for killing fifteen at one blow.*

But the worst was the night of the no-see-ums, flying black specks small enough to get through any opening. Maija-Liisa and I woke up scratching ourselves and crying. Äiti lighted the kerosene lamp and found the ceiling and walls thick with midges that bit until we burned like fire then swelled into red welts that itched even more the more we scratched.]

But off across the tundra, someone else saw the smudge. His head was bald and knobby with bumps that could have been spurs of bone but more likely were welts made by broom handles.

His wife attacked when she was hungry, and after the long winter she was very hungry for tender young things, preferably tender young living things, even more preferably tender young living animal or human things, specifically children of the Lapland or Sami variety.

74

[I shuddered. So did Tonttu.]

With a big black bag dangling from his ape-like arms, the giant lurched across the grass, moving rapidly from rock to rock, hidden from the children by the smoke. Then, as the children centered their attention on the fire, the giant sprang.

["That was Stallo, wasn't it?" Tonttu asked, fully aware of the answer. "Yes." Isä's voice was spectral."]

It was Stallo. Before the children could resist, before they could run, before even Eino could act, they were tumbled into Stallo's bag one by one willy-nilly, and he was dragging them bumping and crying across the rocks toward his hut where his wife had already set a huge cauldron to boil on the hearth."

☽ ○ ✳ ○ ☾

Maija-Liisa was still making circles, searching for wild strawberries under the grass, and Äiti was just far enough away so that she did not interrupt this most bloodthirsty of stories. I could certainly understand why Isä had never told this one before. It was grisly.

"What would you have done if you had been in that bag?" Isä turned to Tonttu.

I sat back and watched him turn to Tonttu. Usually I was the story-teller. I was the one who answered Isä's questions. I was the one who kept the action going.

Yet Isä had turned to Tonttu.

Tonttu mulled over the problem, but not for long. He jumped up and acted out the actions as he said the words: "I would have used my *puukko*." He pulled an imaginary one from a scabbard in his belt. "I would have split the bag open as quick and quiet as could be." He did it, quickly and quietly. "Then I would have grabbed my brothers' and sisters' hands and pulled them out one by one." He reached down into the bag and did so, one by one, counting as he did, keeping one finger to his lips to keep them quiet. When they were all out, he motioned them off on their way and held the *puukko* over Stallo's back.

"Oh, pooh," I burst out. "Eino wouldn't be strong enough to kill a giant with one little knife. That's dumb. And anyway, how could he do all of that when Stallo was awake?"

"Stallo would have stopped to rest."

Well, yes, I tacitly admitted. The bag of children would be heavy even for a giant to carry.

"And as soon as he sat down and nodded off, out they'd go!" Tonttu's eyes sparkled.

"But do you really think that the children could run fast enough to escape Stallo? Giants wear seven-league boots," I scoffed.

"But Eino was smart. He outwitted him. He was smarter even if he wasn't stronger! I know what he did!" The words spilled out all over each other, just like Maija-Liisa's vomit, I thought, but all Isä did was to sit back and smile. "He filled the sack with rocks and fastened it back up again . . . with . . . with . . . some tie from . . . his hat . . . or his belt . . . or his shoes. . . . And when Stallo woke up and picked up the bag, it was just as heavy as it had been before, and he carried it home and opened the bag and dumped the rocks into the cauldron and it boiled over and burned his feet and his wife's feet, and then he was sorry!" Tonttu ended triumphantly.

Isä laughed and leaned over to rumple his hair. Suddenly the two of them were united, caught in a moment of joy by a ray of sunshine that broke through the trees.

And I felt lost and alone.

When Maija-Liisa's clothes were dry enough, Äiti dressed her again; and Isä lifted both of them back into the wagon, Maija-Liisa between them this time, for preventive medicine.

I disdained any help and climbed in myself.

The corduroy road over the worst of the swamp jolted us around some, but I didn't care. We passed through the blueberry fields where the forest fire had been, leading to Dark Lake, but I didn't look to see if the plants had survived the spring frosts. We turned left onto the narrow winding Snake Trail, which jogged erratically toward the Finlander Beach at Lake Leander, and branches switched my head and shoulders, and leaves fell onto my dress, but I didn't feel them.

We unloaded the wagon and joined the other families there already, some neighbors like the Makelas, some relatives and friends from Virginia or Chisholm or Buhl; for this was a half-way point.

I wandered off by myself toward the top of the hill on the other side of the cleared picnic grounds where Risto Raihala had built a small log cabin to use for the summer while he was cutting pulp nearby.

Risto was down with the others, of course, and it was too early for the men to be thirsty. I sat down on the steps.

Then I saw Tonttu, also alone, separate from the others, fishing pole and can of worms in hand, walking out on a fallen dead birch log far enough so he could cast for crappies, and something snapped.

I flew down the gravel path toward the lake heedless of roots and tore my dress in a headlong advance on my enemy. When I reached the log, the words gushed out like the first water from a hand pump, rusty and brackish and brown: "Don't you think you can fool me, Tonttu Victormaki," I screamed.

"No matter how hard you try, you'll never be a part of my family. You'll never be anything but a rotten old Victormaki, just like your dad, mean and cruel. You'll never be anything but an awful awful person who cut off his stepbrother's fingers with an ax. And even your dad couldn't love you. He left, and he left you behind, and I wish you would leave too and go away forever!"

At that, my throat, raspy from the screams, closed and cut off the rest of the tirade. Anger boiled over like the scum on the fish stew. I raced out onto the log and pushed Tonttu Victormaki with all my might. I pushed him into the water.

His eyes had turned red as he listened to me rage, and just before he tottered and fell, he spat back at me: "Neither are you! You're not Isä's daughter any more than I am his son! You're nothing but a bastard he took in! A bastard."

As I gasped and recoiled, I lost my own balance on the slime of the log. Arms flailing, I fell in after him.

At first Tonttu came right up, his boots having found some base in the murky, weedy bottom. When I bobbed up beside him, he spit out a mouthful of water with the word, "Bastard!"

I found a foothold of my own and hit at him screaming with both fists pounding until he went down again.

This time he did not come up.

Isä and Äiti had warned us about the drop-off every time we went to the beach: "It is very near shore. One minute you can feel the lake bottom, and the next you can step off a ledge and go down so deep we could never find you!"

Tonttu did not come up.

My screams of rage turned into sputters as I slipped too and lost my footing, and then the world turned black.

Chapter 12

"Elokuu"

August Aftermath

EVEN NOW, WHEN I LOOK BACK at that time through a softening mist of years, I see it not in shades of white or gray, filagreed with clouds, but like a night sky overladen with the electric energy of a thunder storm. Jagged lightning streaks of pain reverberated in crashing crescendos that rumbled off into the distance only to be replaced by more powerful aftershocks in a cacaphony of destruction, wrought by the gods upon a world—and a girl—grown too saucy. So I had been. Thus I had acted. Forever, it seemed then, I would pay.

Neither Äiti nor Isä nor any of the adults who raced to the beach to find and save us both, not without a considerable expenditure of energy and pain, had heard more than the sound of my screams. What Tonttu had said had blurred into a shrill siren.

I had been the easier to find, my white dress clearly visible even in the blackness of the deep water beyond the drop-off. Moreover, my summer shoes were light as were my undergarments so there was little to weigh me down. My hair was long enough, floating up above me like the fronds of weeds, to provide easy and immediate contact, almost like a rope that simply needed to be towed to the surface then to the bank.

I coughed right away, vomiting up the water I had swallowed, then I lay in a retching wretched pool, infinitely preferring the blackness I had left to the false sunlight around me. I would willingly have suffered the terror and trauma of the water; it was the terror and trauma of the truth Tonttu had spoken that I could not endure.

I could not ask Äiti or Isä about it. I could not ask myself why not.

And for a time Tonttu was far too ill for me to ask him anything.

Isä did find him eventually, but his heavy boots and the weight of his suit pants and the fact that he knew nothing at all about swimming and was terrified of the water complicated his rescue considerably. In fact, when he did finally get a grip on Isä, he came close to drowning both of them with a flailing vise of arm and elbow.

Actually, it was not Isä who ultimately saved Tonttu's life. It was Risto Raihala, the charming wastrel whose languid, dark eyes were to be the downfall of many an innocent in the years to come. Then, he was relatively innocent of the ways of the world. But he had been to town several times, and he was a talker. Thus, in one way or another, either in person or vicariously, he had had a lot of experiences for a boy not yet fifteen years old.

He had moved out of his family home about the same time as two of his older brothers had wounded each other seriously in a knife fight and not long after Simonsonin Tuppu had disappeared completely during a fall hunting trip taken with the eldest of the Raihala boys.

Tuppu's body was never found, his fate remaining a mystery, much discussed even long after all of his partners had been forgotten. Word had it that he had been stuffed into a well-box somewhere.

But it was not Risto who was at fault, that was for sure. Of them all, he was the least dangerous . . . at least with a knife. In other ways . . . well . . . later he was to marry well, a woman of substance who owned her own resort.

Later, rumor had it that he was worse than useless as a resort owner. He wouldn't notice if a light bulb were burned out or know how to change it even if he did, a friend was once to say with a shake of his head and a grin. Most people grinned when they talked to or about Risto. A worker, he was not. A charmer, he was always to be, even until he died.

But neither he nor Tonttu died that day. When Tonttu pulled Isä down for a third and, it seemed, the final time during a fruitless attempt to calm him and bring him to shore, Risto dived in, reached the floundering pair, grabbed Tonttu by the shirt collar, no longer starchy, socked him on the jaw so hard that everyone on shore heard the crack, then hauled him ignominiously in by the hair.

Risto was so incensed that, when he got to shore, in typically Raihala fashion, he laid the boy, who was by then not breathing at all, over his knees and whacked him with all his might wherever he could reach. Some of the blows hit his butt but others ricocheted up into his back area. Finally water gushed out, and Tonttu breathed again, and Risto got control of himself, faster than a Raihala normally would, and quit whacking.

When Tonttu breathed and it was clear that he would live, he was totally unable to control the tremors that shook his body or the tears that tore from his very soul. He knew, although no one else did except me, that he had committed a second unforgivable act: he had hurt another child, quite as cruelly as he had Verner, and with equal awareness and intent. What he had said—the truth as he saw it—concerned him less than that he had divulged information

79

not his to know or to pass along to others. It was gossip, pure and simple, vicious gossip of the kind that his father had fed upon in a sick and bloated way.

When Tonttu's mother had called for Äiti, beset by the travail of the birth of the child whose death and hers had ensued no matter the effort to save them, Mr. Victormaki had scoffed, "Why would you want that bitch, that holier-than-thou, sanctimonious hypocrite here? She's no better than she should be. You know God damn well that that first kid is not her husband's.

"I saw her at the lumber camp in Floodwood where she worked before she ever met him, and she had swallowed a watermelon seed that had already grown into size. That kid was born before she ever met the man she calls her husband, who calls himself the kid's father. That kid is nothing but a bastard, and the woman is nothing but a slut, and I won't have her in my house." Then he had gone, slamming the door behind him, and Tonttu's mother had been left writhing on the bed, crying, wailing, moaning with pain, begging for succor.

It had been Tonttu, finally, who had crept out the door and across the field and asked Äiti please, please-to-come-because-his-mother-was-bleeding-and-the-baby-wouldn't-come-and-now-she-wasn't-even-trying-and-would-Äiti-please-help?

It had taken Tonttu's mother, the first Mrs. Victormaki, two days to die, although the hemorrhage had made the end inevitable.

The baby, too, despite their attempts to feed it with an eyedropper and pack it in wool and keep it in the warming oven, had succumbed.

Mr. Victormaki had sworn, "Good riddance." She had been a weak, mealy-mouthed mistake for a wife, he said. As soon as the funeral was over and he could hitch up a horse, he had headed for Soudan to find a replacement.

The second Mrs. Victormaki of the Titian hair and the musical fingers on the *kantele* and the gentle manner had not, however, come unencumbered. In fact, it may well have been for Verner's sake that she had accepted the blunt proposal of the man who seemed rough and crude yet offered her the safety of what he called a good home.

Verner needed a home. Two alternatives lay open to her—an honorable marriage or a dishonorable alliance.

She was not strong enough to cook at a lumber camp, although she had tried mightily. She had been fired both for inciting the crew to violent actions by her lascivious looks and for burning the bread and pies three days in a row.

That the crew had attempted . . . over-familiarity, she later explained delicately to Äiti . . . after surreptitious consumption of quarts of moonshine and that the wood for the woodstove was wet were excuses not to be brooked.

She was not educated enough to teach, not having attended school in Finland before her family emigrated, and not learned enough to read or write or even to speak English until after they settled in Canada.

She was not able to find work as a maid or cook or governess, even in the larger city of Duluth, without commensurate evening responsibilities to the young men of the house, which she was loathe to endure.

In short, her choice had been simple—Mr. Victormaki or starvation, not just for her, but for Verner, her son, not by marriage, it was heavily hinted, but by a misalliance in her mysterious past.

Äiti had done everything she could to take the second Mrs. Victormaki under her wing and help her toward community acceptance. But in the background lurked another truth, and Äiti feared Mr. Victormaki, feared him with good reason.

She knew he had known her before. She knew he had visited the lumber camp in Floodwood. And she did not trust him, not for a moment. He would hoard his small stock of scandal jealously, never spending it for naught. He would save it until it would stand him well.

He would never have guessed that it would not be he who used it. It would be his son. Nor could Mr. Victormaki ever have guessed that once the facts were out, his son would be so overcome with remorse that it, even more than the near drowning, kept him submerged in a depression and lethargy equivalent to my own. Not only had he hurt me. He had also spoken ill of the one person whose kindness had never failed. He had besmirched her name. He had spoken the unspeakable, and the words could not be taken back.

Thus, as I retreated behind walls of pain, he retreated behind walls of regret. We both suffered to the point of physical illness, which was attributed at first, of course, to the accident.

We both maintained stoic silence on that score—except for each of us assuming the blame—earning much praise for our forbearance, enduring thereby qualms of added regret for living an outright lie. But neither of us could bear to talk about it, not I because I could not bear to face what I perceived to be the truth, not Tonttu because he could not explain. What he had said was all he knew.

The only one who suffered more than we was Maija-Liisa; for the anger that I had previously expended toward Tonttu, the absymal depths of the hatred I had felt for him, I unwittingly transferred in part to her.

I was not Isä's daughter. She was.
I was not Äiti's and Isä's child. She was.
I was a bastard. She was legitimate.
I was bad. She was good.

Thus, I found myself treating her much as Tonttu had once treated Verner, with cruel distaste and utter envy.

Nor could I any longer solace myself with dreams of the birth money. It, too, was besmirched, tangible evidence that I was different, that I was an outsider, that whoever and wherever I had come from, they had paid Äiti and paid me to stay away, never to return. It was not, I thought, birth money. It was guilt money. It was dirty, filthy, distance money.

It was blood money, designed to keep the soiled blood in my body separate from, far away from, the body from which it had originated, a body which clearly wanted nothing to do with me, wanted no part of my life, had denied me sharing its identity.

Thus, I had no identity.

Later I looked up the word "bastard" in the English-Finnish dictionary. It said that I had been "begotten and born of an illicit union." Then I looked up "illicit." It said that I was "improper, unlawful, not permitted or allowed."

But, at that time, I needed no dictionary to define how I felt. I knew. I should not even be. I should have died in the water. I should, in fact, be gone, be dead, be somewhere, anywhere else. I was not a proper person; I had somehow broken the law. I was not to be permitted or allowed . . . what? To live? To be a part of a family?

Torn and ravaged with questions, I snapped at Maija-Liisa. I refused to help her when she asked. I pushed her aside when Äiti wasn't looking. I held myself as far away from her as I could in bed, even when she was cold and needed cuddling as she almost always did. I quit telling her stories. In fact, I quit speaking to her at all.

But then, I had also quit speaking to Äiti and Isä.

I had locked myself into a trunk much more confining than the one which held Äiti's secrets, for I knew that I was one of the secrets, and it was there that I too should have been kept. For a long time, that was how I lived—in a bleak, black silence, alone and unresponsive to any stimuli. When Isä tried to kiss or carry or hold me, I slipped out of his arms or squeezed away. When Äiti touched me, soothed me as she braided my hair, or tried to talk, I sat stiffly starched in front of her and adopted Tonttu's monosyllabic *"joo" eli "eia." Yes* or *no* were the standard responses.

I quit eating altogether.

And mostly quit sleeping too.

I could not allow myself even the surcease of escape into the Hölömöläiset family's misadventures. I hated them, too. For all their troubles, they too were a family. They stuck together. They were as one; what happened to one involved them all.

How unaware could I be that what was happening to me also involved others? Äiti and Isä, of course, unbeknownst to me, locked in my own prison of Chillon, were spending days and nights plotting rescue. Had I but known, I would have smiled; for Isä did all but don armor and shield in his attempts to circumvent the dragon that had captured me. One of his key weapons, of course, was the Hölömöläiset, who, it seemed, always stood at the ready, willing to appear when needed, with a relevant experience.

But since Isä did not know exactly what was wrong, he was not sure what was relevant.

Early one evening, exhausted from the day but not quite ready to sit down to supper, we collapsed on the back stoop. He drew Maija-Liisa onto his lap and, as she settled back, spoke ostensibly to her but in fact to all of us in a voice as soft and cool as the evening breeze.

I held myself rigidly apart, hating him for holding her, hating her for fitting there, hating myself for hating them, hating Tonttu and even Äiti. But I could not help but hear and there was nowhere for me to go.

"Many years ago, many hundred years ago, perhaps in the very earliest days, when the long night of winter was ended and the light and glory of summer returned to the land, the people of Finland, in their gladness, went out into the forests and to the lakes that they loved so well and spent a day in merrymaking, in rejoicing that the winter was past and the summer had come. Thus grew up *Juhannus*, Midsummer's Day."

The recitative tone of Isä's voice made it clear that these words were not his. They had come to him, along with the words of the *Kalevala*, from a time long ago, from a place long gone, from a storyteller lost in a dream. But that was no matter. The sound and the beat were calming.

Maija-Liisa was enraptured, not so much by the words as by the sounds. She, who never could tell stories, was all her life to listen with great joy to Isä's and to mine.

Tonttu, who had been trying futilely over the last few days to figure out how to make her a doll out of a corn husk, set one more fruitless attempt aside and gently took the bushel basket of freshly-picked ears of corn from in front of Äiti and indicated with a nod his willingness to finish the real husking job himself. It would give him an excuse to listen.

I felt the words flow around me, drawing me in whether I wanted them to or not. We were sitting on the steps in the late afternoon of the first day of fall. Oh, it was still August—*Elokuu*—by the calendar, but the wind was blowing crisp and fresh. The sky vibrated with blue, and the air felt tangy and cool, like a green apple, not quite ripe but tasty and refreshing.

Isä and Tonttu had scythed and stacked the last of the hay into the pole barn, where it could dry for winter storage. I had been directed to hill potatoes one last time, a back-breaking task that left me, by supper, so worn from plain hard work that it was difficult to muster up the usual barricade of silent resentment.

Isä had shot the first partridge he had allowed us since the season for mating and brooding and raising the young ones, and Äiti had stuffed it with the last of the previous year's wild rice and put it into the oven to bake slowly.

The dressing combined wild rice with herbs and bits of salt pork and onion, sauteed in butter, moistened with fresh cream.

New potatoes I had picked from the hills where the vines had been wilted and dry for weeks were boiling gently on the stove, to be mixed with butter and parsley.

And a big pot of water had been set back from the firebox far enough to hold the heat but not the boil until we were ready to drop the corn in.

Even I considered it a sumptuous feast, further garnished with fresh quick bread into which Äiti had mixed grated zucchini.

My stomach growled, and I knew that I would try to eat that night. I did, in fact, often make the attempt. But the moment before dinner when we all held hands and someone said grace usually did me in. Symbolically at that moment, we were linked in love. Of all of the moments of the day, that one was usually the hardest for me to bear.

But that day, it was the Hölömöläiset who enhanced my private agony even as they offered me escape:

☽ ○ ✴ ○ ☾

ON THAT VERY SPECIAL DAY, the ship fitted, the reindeer boarded, and the stores packed for the journey, the children having escaped from Stallo, the Hölömöläiset were prepared to set sail. But instead of unfurling the sails, as Ahti had suggested, most tactfully but in a strong captain's voice, Father Jussi paused. He had an alternate plan: "*Lapset,* children," he roared in his quietest voice, "*Istu.* Sit down. I have a plan."

The children nodded, willingly hunkering down in a circle around him. They were always ready when he had a plan.

"Today be a special day." He paused to see if they were listening.

They were.

"Today all Finnish peoples celebrate sunshine. Today all Finnish peoples honor summer. Today all Finnish peoples celebrate Finland. We not leave till it be over. We celebrate dis one las' time. We celebrate being Finn."

The children did not quite understand the word "celebrate." But they loved the sunshine and the summer, and deep in their hearts they loved Finland. It would be hard to leave the land behind—the tundra, the lakes, the trees, the wide and open sky.

"We take the old wagon-cart that we used when we traveled in the summer."

"*Joo,*" the children nodded again. They knew the cart well and had grieved some at having it too left behind.

"Poys, you go cut birch branches, as many as you c'n find. Make 'em fresh, mind you, not dry ones that've fallen. Be sure they've leaves upon 'em."

The boys nodded. They drew out their *puukkos.* Eino and the twins checked the blades of their axes. They were sharp.

"*Tyttö*—Girls," Father Jussi tried to speak even more softly, to indicate that this would be pleasurable work leading to pleasurable moments. Thus, he growled. "You gather hay, soft hay, fresh hay. You will know it be fresh in four ways."

The girls fixed their eyes upon his enormous hand, showing four fingers, one twisted from a battle with a recalcitrant reindeer.

"One. It be green."

"Green." The girls nodded.

One finger went down.

"Two. It be soft. If you step on it or sit on it, it not prickle."

"Soft." The girls nodded. No prickle.

One more finger went down.

"Three. When you close your eyes, it smell sweet, like honey."

"Sweet." The girls twitched their noses and nodded. Like honey.

One more finger went down.

Father Jussi continued, his fourth finger descending rapidly, "Four. Tasty. The sweet inside core will taste as good to you as it will, in the winter, to the reindeer."

[*Tonttu could not repress a snicker, and he and Isä shared a man-look. I shot each one a disparaging glance. Äiti's similarly reproving look met mine, and she smiled, tentatively, a woman-look indicating forbearance. I tried not to, but a very small smile flickered back. Isä noticed it but did not comment. He grinned and continued.*]

"Tasty." The girls licked their lips and nodded.

"Now, off you go, you *lapset,* and don't come back till you be ready!" Father Jussi boomed in a whisper.

And off they went.

They did not come back until they were ready. By then, it was evening, but the night had not come. The sky was alight, flashing and shining with beacons, streaking gold like the sun and green and blue, like firelight, misplaced, or fireworks, coming from parts unknown.

The children looked up, awed, grateful to be there to see the sight.

Then, the boys laid the birch branches all across the bottom of the cart until it was padded well, and atop them the girls spread the sweet, soft hay.

Father Jussi had placed two wooden stools in the corners of the cart, and to one he led Mummu Hölömöläinen with great respect and due ceremony. Once she was seated, he spread his great arms, told her and the children all to close their eyes, and from nowhere magically sprang a great surprise.

It was the fiddler, come to share their celebration.

The children stared wide-eyed at the scrawny bent shape of a tiny man, his head bald except for a fringe of brownish gray hair as stiff as dried hay stalks, with a fiddle and a bow in his hands. Then they caught Mummu's eye and showed their good manners by bowing (boys) and curtsying prettily (girls).

The fiddler bowed back with grace and reverence, less to them, however, than to Mummu, who, it must be admitted, was glowing as sweet and fresh herself as if she had been one of the girls instead of the mother.

Then he climbed into the corner of the cart, sat down on the other stool, and the bow hit the fiddle.

And the children learned the meaning of the word "celebrate."

So did the reindeer, for they pulled away with a will, and the cart jounced joyously down the path to the music of the dances the fiddler played, waltzes and polka and schottisches, mixed with songs so bright and happy that the wind itself danced to the tunes. And the sun stayed awake to listen.

And after a time, they came to a meadow, a clearing in the forest where a Maypole had been raised.

[*"What is a Maypole?" Maija-Liisa asked, excited, her eyes sparkling.*

"It is the trunk of a tree, shorn of branches and leaves, with wide colored ribbons fastened to the very top, ribbons so long that they trail from the top of the tree to the ground and curl upon the grass in swirls of blue and green, yellow and red, even orange, indigo, and violet, a rainbow of colors as lucent in the dark as the northern stars, alight with the glimmering tails of fireflies, flashing around the field."

"Ooohhh," Maija-Liisa barely breathed the word.

Even I, who was trying hard again to remain distant, sighed at the beauteous image.]

Then Father Jussi lifted the girls down, one by one, starting with Mummu, who flushed pink at the kiss he dropped on her forehead, and to each he gave one ribbon from the tree. With a gesture he indicated that they were to stand there, quietly, to wait.

The boys lifted the fiddler and his stool from the cart, so as not to interrupt his playing, and ran to gather firefies, which served well as lanterns if they were contained.

When even the littlest, Vieno . . . [*Isä nodded and smiled at Äiti, who blushed and nodded and smiled back.*] . . . when even Vieno was standing, ribbon in hand, the girls began to move in a circle. Mummu Hölömöläinen knew the steps, and they followed her as she danced behind the girls as far away from the pole as the ribbon would reach. Twirling once, she glided forward, back, to the right and again; forward, back, to the right, in a tripping, skipping rhythm that flowed faster and faster. The girls joined in, slowly first and then faster until even Vieno was flowing with the ribbons in a circle around the tree.

The boys sighed at the wonder of it, and Father Jussi looked proud.

Then, at some secret signal, the girls began to weave among each other so that the ribbons wove, too, in and out and around, in and out and around, making the circle smaller and smaller, until the ribbons and the tree and the dancers melded together, and the music ended, and the night was still.

For a long moment, the boys sat silent too. Then, overcome with a need to express their praise, they clapped their hands together and stood and whistled and clapped some more until the pinewoods reverberated the sound back to them, echoing their applause. And the sun blinked, and the lights of the Northland streamed across the sky their own ribands of joy.

Father Jussi nodded and smiled, and the fiddler nodded and smiled.

It was a night without slumber, a night of celebration.

It was the night the Hölömöläiset said farewell forever to Finland.

"How could they bear to leave?" I burst out, having leaned forward inadvertently and unaware, caught by the magic.

Maija-Liisa, silent through the narrative, enthralled, at the end burrowed her face into her Isä's shoulder and burst into tears.

Äiti too wiped her eyes.

Tonttu looked away. He could not show his feelings.

But I could not cry. I sat, frozen by the knowledge that the happy days were over for the Hölömöläiset. They would come to Amerika, and here their magic would end. Here they too would find deer instead of reindeer, harsh winter, stubborn land, and truths that hurt.

Like the Hölömöläiset, I had known summer. But I had not known I knew until it was gone. I had understood what it meant to celebrate. But I had not known I knew until it was too late.

"How could they bear to leave?" I repeated.

"They could not bear to stay," Äiti answered. "They knew that it was time to go."

They knew that it was time.

And so did I.

It was time for truth. But unlike the Hölömöläiset, I lacked the courage to act. Instead, the floodgates burst. The locks of the weir opened, and the tears came, storms of tears rent with thunder and lightning, fraught with terror and danger, strife and pain.

Of them all it was, ironically, Tonttu who reached for me first and held back the winds that threatened to carry me too far away from all I loved, who enfolded me in strong warm arms, keeping me safe until the storm ebbed.

Äiti could not. She was crying with me, heavy tears than ran from her heart although she was not quite sure why. Isä could not. He was crying with me, quiet man tears that oozed from under the stone that had lain upon them and upon his heart for all the years of my life and months more.

But Finnish men never cry so he got up and walked away.

Suddenly, the process by which I had come to knowledge became unimportant. In one flash of the heart's lightning, I quit blaming Tonttu for my pain. I could not share my knowledge yet. I could not understand who I was or why. But I knew that what I was was not Tonttu's fault. His words had cut me with the force of a sharp and deadly *puukko*. But I could forgive him that. As he had sinned against Verner and me, I had sinned against him.

And, truth be told, against Maija-Liisa, too.

Had I also sinned against Äiti and Isä? Whose in truth was the sin?

I was not ready to leave, like the Hölömöläiset. I had no father to make a plan. All I had at that time was Tonttu, who shared the knowledge and the pain. For a time, he was enough.

Chapter 13

"Isotalon Antti"

IDON'T KNOW WHAT WOULD HAVE HAPPENED the night that I cried, whether in the long run it all would have been resolved immediately and perhaps therefore more easily, had there not just then been a knock on the door.

We all jumped.

Visitors were not exactly unexpected, especially during the spring and the summer. They came walking down the road usually about suppertime heading toward the Rainy Lake spur railroad that ran from Leander to Jacksons' swamp.

The Rainy Lake Mill, which operated out of Virginia, had sent their timber cruisers north years ago. They had found not only the major timber claims past Orr near Cusson but several stands of virgin pine nearby between Jacksons and Makelas. Isä had brought us to see stumps so wide that two men could not put their arms around their five-foot diameter. We liked to stop at the camp where the lumberjacks and their cook gave us cookies and dough-nuts.

Early that summer, now that the Cusson camps were also open, it was not uncommon for lumberjack *jibbos* to come walking by and stop to ask, "Any *vettä*, water, to drink?"

Isä always said, "Sure. Have all you want. But would you like butter-milk?"

Äiti could have made money on her fresh buttermilk if she had want-ed to. She never did although she did accept any news about friends in town most willingly. But her kindness reaped its own reward, for sometimes on their way back to town, work completed or camp closed, those same men would ask Isä, "Need any help?" Thus we had been able to build two barns, one between our house and the Victormakis, one toward Makelas, *"heinä lato,"* hay barns with roofs of birchbark, shingled and tight. They were full by late August. We did not need any more hay than Isä and Tonttu had already reaped and stored for Dolly.

But just before the storms came earlier in the month, all of the neighbor men had gathered to make sure the hay in the Victormaki pastures did not go to waste.

None of the womenfolk had ever liked Mr. Victormaki, that was for sure, nor perhaps did the men. But he had helped each one of them, they all remembered, when help was needed, and he had been the only one with a horse other than the one Makelas had staked at Lake Leander during the previous summer's tornado.

Starting out, none of the immigrant farmers would have survived without Mr. Victormaki's horse and his strength. He could work in his own fields full power for eight to ten hours at a stretch, eat supper, then head out to help a neighbor for another five or six hours until the sun set.

For some, that help had made the difference.

When Mr. Victormaki had left, therefore, so abruptly, late that winter, the neighbor men had united to preserve his homestead, dividing the cattle among them, and now harvesting the hay field that would otherwise have begun a reclamation project, for that which is nature's will speedily take back that which is man's.

By early August, all of the hay barns were full—ours and the Victormakis—secure from rain, the hay drying, in part thanks to those vagabond *jibbos*. But we had had no visitors for a long time, the large camps having closed until winter ice and snow could pack the roads and freeze the lakes for easy access to the timber and easier hauling out. Only small neighborhood camps stayed open, stockpiling for later sale.

Thus, when we heard the knock on the door, we were startled and not a little concerned. Late-night visitors usually carried with them either bad news or trouble.

That night, however, Isä opened the door to . . . Stallo!

We were amazed. Amazed to see Isä embrace him and he, Isä. Amazed that after a brief initial shrinking from the enormous form which filled the entire doorway, Äiti too sprang up, tears forgotten, to hug and even kiss this stranger, the biggest man we had ever seen.

Of course he saw us shrinking in the lea, and when the first furor of greeting had abated, he looked right at us. We sat transfixed until we heard his voice—low, deep, but unmistakably gentle. It rumbled like thunder but without lightning, erupted like a volcano without lava, spewed like a rapids without rocks.

Although we feared his size, we could not fear that voice, the utterance of a creative rather than a destructive force.

"*Sanoa*—say—'hallo' to Isotalon Antti," he said to us.

His name was a singular and interesting contradiction in terms. "*Iso*" means tall. A "*talo*" is a house. Thus, he was Antti of the Big House, surname first by Finnish tradition.

That made me smile, for having heard who he was even I remembered the story: he lived in a house so small that as Lehti Aapo had often said, to get out frontwards you had to go in backwards.

"*Haluatko kahvia?*—Do you want any coffee?" Äiti asked, setting out the partridge and dressing and vegetables and bread kept warm on the back of the stove.

Somehow, in some strange way, Isotallon Antti brought us all back from the Stygian place where our souls had flown to a facade as high as the square fronts of the stores in Cook, false like them, yet serving well as a mask.

Asea on the flow of small talk and the backwash of gossip, Maija-Liisa and I floated until we had eaten our fill and nodded ourselves to a drowsy stupor over our plates and been disrobed and set to sleep unbeknownst. Thus, that which could have been a time of revelation became a time of blessed rest, and we all awoke in the morning refreshed in body if still somewhat bestirred by emotional undercurrents.

At breakfast, the big man caught us by surprise once more. When Äiti's and Isä's backs were turned, he drew a finger the size of a .22 revolver to his lips and whispered, "I don't know what nationality they are, but I've been feeding bits of hardtack to some little bits of men who have been following me." He paused and barely breathed the word—"Elves!"

That was the end of breakfast for us. When he headed outside, booted knees rising high then dropping softly in the masquerade of a march, we followed him like the Pied Piper's rats, Tonttu, then me, then Maija-Liisa. Out the back door we went, single file, our knees lifted too, in slow motion.

"Shhhh," he turned to warn us, his finger to his lips again.

We shushed the sounds we hadn't been making.

Down the path we pranced, one behind the other, in a parody of a parade, past the sauna and toward the barn. Near the barn sat the wagon, a sack on the seat for a cushion.

"There's one now! On that sack!" His voice echoed like a buffalo herd in stampede.

We stopped in our tracks.

There was absolutely nothing on the sack.

Later that day he saw snakes, too, where there were none, on the clean clear path to the house.

Isotalon Antti left before supper, holding a pounding head fast to his shoulders to make sure that it went where he went.

Isä shook his head when he saw him leave: the sack on his back was clinking suspiciously.

It had been full of half-pints of moon, some of which Harjun Kassu made on his own still, much of which had been smuggled in via a booze-runner cheap from Canada or had been delivered in fifty-gallon jugs via the underground from Superior.

We cried to see him leave even though there hadn't been elves or snakes. He had offered an entertaining distraction.

Isä looked askance at our disappointment. "You should know better than to listen to a fool like that." But he too had been taken in over and over again by this smooth talker from Soudan. Isotalon Antti knew how to get what he wanted, that was for sure, be it a bed for the night or a dinner or a jar of buttermilk or a goodly supply of moon, and he had no compunction about packing in other things he needed. Several loaves of bread and a freshly smoked haunch of venison had padded the bottles in that sack, and two perfectly good clean horse blankets had also disappeared from the barn.

He had almost sweet-talked us into seeing what wasn't there.

He had sweet-talked Äiti into not seeing what was.

Isotalon Antti never did come back.

That was fine with me. Yet whether he did or not was immaterial, for I would never gainsay him a welcome. He had given all of us a vision far clearer than anything he could conjure up out of words or signs or moon. He had given us distance from our problems and a dream, however delusive, to pursue for a time. Of such is survival made, I was later to realize. Distance and dreams hone the edges of the sharpest knife, buffing it to a more malleable form. So they did that day.

By the next morning after Stallo's leaving, we had had twenty-four hours of respite. We had needed every minute.

"That reminds me of a Hölömöläiset story," Isä mused as we had watched the big man weaving down the road in the late afternoon, marching to the beat of his own drum.

We trailed after him to hear the story as we carried wood for the sauna stove and water for washing, as we swept the floor and shook the rugs. Although preparing the sauna was usually the men's job, we all worked together that night, getting in each other's way a bit and, Maija-Liisa especially, dropping as much wood and spilling as much water as she carried. But the story, though told episodically whenever we converged, hung together remarkably well and for once seemed to serve no ulterior motive. Like Isotalon Antti's imaginings, it simply entertained us.

Sᴛᴀʟʟᴏ ᴛʜᴇ Gɪᴀɴᴛ, ᴛᴏᴏ, was apt to imbibe when given the opportunity, When worse came to worse, he drank milk fermented with reindeer blood.

[*"Yuck," we said, horrified, and shook the rugs hard.*]

When the burns on his feet had healed, he drank all that was left in the stone crocks and swore revenge on the Hölömöläiset children.

[*"Oh, dear," I thought. "I hope he knows when to stop." I had renounced revenge. Whatever bad names Tonttu had called me when he was angry, I had deserved them. I had treated him very poorly in my desire for revenge. Now, rested and restored, I wondered that I had taken his words so to heart and regretted the extent to which I had allowed words spoken in anger to govern my actions. Why, of course Isä was my father. He had always been there, ever since I could remember; and in every possible way he had showed me that he was mine and I his. Why, we even looked alike—though my eyes were green to his blue—with big noses and upper lips a bit too long, definite chins, and high prominent cheekbones.*]

[*Thus for a time I embroidered the designs on the fabric of my fool's paradise.*]

[*Tonttu, on the other hand, from a first-hand vantage, solemnly considered the reality of revenge: "What did Stallo do?" he asked, meditatively.*]

First, he packed his tools—a hammer. Nails. Pliers. A rope. Five knives of varying sizes, knives he had made himself out of steel blades, honing and sharpening them to enhance an edge as strong as it was lethal. Then he swathed his wife in strips of clean rags and cheesecloth and slung her over his shoulder, and the two set out along the path that led to the pirate ship.

[*I shivered in a pretense of horror and sat down on the lavat, the benches in the sauna dressing room. Tonttu let himself drop onto the clean rug on the floor and spread himself out wide. Maija-Liisa curled by beside him. Isä stoked the fire in the sauna kiuas, added one more birch log, and joined the rest of us to wait for the rocks to heat up.*]

When they reached the shore near the pirate ship, Stallo hunched over to make himself as small as he could and whined, "Help us! Help us! My wife is sick, and I am hungry, and we have lost our home. I have repented my sins and seek forgiveness. Help these weary travelers! Help us, kind friends."

Just as they always did when called, the Hölömöläiset boys lined up, this time along the starboard bow:

First Eino, the oldest;
then Urho and Matti,
then Toivo and Sulo, the twins,
Onnie, Pekka, and Kalle,
and Ahti, the sailor,
and Severi, last of those Finns.

"You can't fool us, Stallo!" they cried. "We know who you be!"

"And that sack on your back will not hold any of the Hölömöläiset ever, ever again," Father Jussi roared from a highpoint on the mizzenmast.

"Never ever again," the boys echoed across the water.

"But the sack on my back holds my sick wife," Stallo whimpered, "and I suffer agonies, too! Take pity upon us, and give us some supper, and blessings will fall upon you!"

Now that caused the Hölömöläiset some pause. Mummu had often said that kindness to others rebounds into blessings. It had been true of the forest animals whom the Hölömöläiset had loved and protected and who, in turn, had kept them from freezing during the long, cold winter.

"If we help you, will you promise not to bring any weapons aboard?" Father Jussi was thinking ahead.

"I carry none," Stallo insisted. "All that I have on my belt are tools. I will use them to help you. I am stalwart and strong. I am so tall I can reach to the top of the masts. I will fasten your sails with my rope. I will pull the barnacles off the keel with my pliers. All that I ask is some food for my wife and perhaps just a pittance for me."

His words had the ring of truth, and they were true, as far as they went.

The Hölömöläiset boys were sure that they knew truth when they heard it: "Oh, come aboard, Stallo. We'll feed you and help you. And we will forgive you your sins," they said.

Only Mummu turned her head slightly and narrowed her eyes. Truth was all right as far as truth went. But sometimes it was important that it also be fact.

Father Jussi, however, agreed with the boys. "Joo," he said.

"Joo," cried the girls, who had been listening from the poop deck.

"Joo," Mummu capitulated.

So Stallo jumped into the water, and pushing the sack ahead of him, he swam to the ship and climbed in.

[*"Why were the Hölömöläiset so foolish?" I wondered aloud. "They should have known better than to trust anything he said."*

"Don't we all sometimes hear what we want to hear and believe what we want to believe and trust that in general people are honest?" Isä asked me.

I did not want to answer that question.]

All that day Stallo worked. First, he used the pliers to pry all of the barnacles off of the keel. But in the process he also pulled out every single peg holding the keel-boards together. Only the pressure of the water kept them in place. Then he climbed to the topgallant sails and roped on the sails and hammered and nailed them securely . . . so securely that they would never drop down. Never would those sails fill with wind and propel the ship forward. They were irrevocably lashed to the masts.

And Stallo still had the five knives.

[*"Where had he hidden them?" Tonttu asked eagerly.*

"Where would you have hidden them?" Isä asked all three of us.

"I would push them into the sides of my boots," I answered. I had seen a puukko *peeking from Risto Raihala's boots more than once.*

"Joo," Isä nodded. "The boots would hold two knives. What about the other three?"

"He could hide one in his hat, if it were little," Tonttu suggested.

"Joo. Three. And the other two?"

"I'll bet his wife had them! I'll bet she was going to use them to carve the smallest Hölömöläiset children into packable pieces to smoke for the winter!" It made sense to me, in view of her propensity for tender young things.

"Joo." Isä approved.

Maija-Liisa shuddered, in light of her still being a tender young thing.]

When darkness finally fell, late, as it did on those last warm summer days, the Hölömöläiset children and Mummu and Father Jussi each rolled into a hammock slung below deck in the hold. They gave Stallo and his wife the cabin beds since they were the guests.

[*"The Hölömöläiset didn't just go to sleep!" I was as appalled by their credulity as I was by Stallo's duplicity.*

"What do you think?" Isä asked predictably.

We stared at him, wide-eyed.]

Late, late in the night, when the fireflies were asleep and the northern lights had flickered and died, Stallo and his wife crept out of the cabin toward the hammocks where the Hölömöläiset slept. Stallo slid his *puukkos* out of his boots and hat, and Stallo's wife held hers high, one in each hand. Closer and closer to the hammocks they crept.

Then they jumped.

[*Maija-Liisa jumped, too. So, it must be admitted, did Tonttu and I.*]

But . . . [*Isä's voice rose triumphantly*], so did the Hölömöläiset! They were not in their hammocks at all but hiding all around the edges of the hold, waiting.

Before Stallo and his wife could move again, the Hölömöläiset had wound them tightly into ropes. Ahti tied the ropes with sailors' knots, and they carried the two up onto the deck."

[*"Then what did they do?" we breathed.*

"What would you do?"

We were ready: "We would pull up the anchor and tie them to it and drop it into the water again with Stallo and his wife attached, and that would be the end of them for once and for all."]

They pulled up the anchor and tied them to it and dropped it into the water again with Stallo and his wife attached, and that was the end of them for once and for all, [*Isä concluded, to our great satisfaction.*]

The tales of the Hölömöläiset may have been as apocryphal as Isotalon Antti's elves, but to us it was not important that they be factual, just that they be true. In our minds, the Hölömöläiset lived.

It was not until the following morning that we chose to face a reality that they and Isotalon Antti and the elves and our tears had, in sequence, washed away for a time.

Unfortunately that reality was both true and factual, and there was no denying it.

$$\text{☽ ○ ✴ ○ ☾}$$

Chapter 14

"Marraskuu"

November,
When Winter Comes Early

THE CATHARTIC NATURE OF THE TEARS and the normalcy with which we had interacted with Isotalon Antti had masked the reality of the situation for Isä and Äiti especially.

It may have been—I can see in retrospect through the vantage of years—that they simply wanted it so. Be that as it may, neither adult perceived how Tonttu and I truly felt, for children we still were and not that much older than Maija-Liisa even in years. We were children in spite of the demands placed upon us to share the endless work tasks that had to be completed for a family to survive in that as yet unconquered wilderness.

Children then grew up faster than they do now and matured into adulthood earlier. Not in the way they dressed. Not in the jewelry they wore. Not in the amount of privilege they enjoyed. But in the amount of adult responsibility they faced, knew, and accepted as needful.

Barely had I learned the elements of washing clothes before I became a wash-day partner. For all my life the scar from the burn would offer mute testimony to my role on ironing day.

And Tonttu, since he had been old enough to walk, had shared in the barn work; for he was the oldest of the Victormaki children.

Of all the children born to a pioneer family, it was always the oldest who had to grow up the fastest. The first, simple, universally immutable law of family then, a law as irreversible as the force of gravity, was that parents needed help.

The fathers who were trying to wrest a farm and fields from a recalcitrant land covered with trees and rocks needed extra hands, which they could not afford to hire. They were grateful for the some-time help of men like Lehti Aapo, but that on-again-off-again, here-today-gone-tomorrow assistance was woefully inadequate. So too were the capacities of the mothers, no matter the strength of their will.

Since every fire built demanded wood cut, split, carried, and piled, it was no wonder that the Makelas were sometimes reduced to keeping the door to the wood stove open and to pushing in the end of the log as it burned down. The house may have been smokey, but it was warm. They survived.

Such compromises between the way the women wanted their homes to be and the way they often were had their own consequences, of course. Mrs. Makela, for instance, whose eyes had never been strong, found their condition exacerbated by the pungency of the wood smoke that permeated everything in their house. At first, her eyes simply stung and ached and watered all the time. But increasingly, she found herself sensitive to all forms of light, whatever the level of brightness; and then, she confided to Äiti, she began to feel as if there were sand under her eyelids. Äiti brought her our eye cup, and they washed both eyes carefully with a mild boric acid solution, but the sand would not wash out. Then came days and weeks when she saw thin metallic silvery banners flying in circles around the periphery of her vision. And finally, a sea of black gnats floated across the eye itself, and a shade came down.

The Makelas did not have enough money to consult Dr. Hicks. Kastren Papa came and prescribed a time of rest in a dark, cool room and cool cloths across the eyes and a tincture of laudanum, no more than twenty-five drops in a day, to help her relax and to mitigate the pain, which was ultimately to become so excruciating that she paced the floor day and night trying not to scream. She held Äiti's hand so tightly that it hurt and whispered that every time she blinked it felt as if she were running a flat iron down her eyeball.

Äiti cried for her. But there was no hope. How could Mrs. Makela lie down with five little ones to care for and a sixth on the way?

No wonder Sophie Seraphina, who was just my age, never had time to play. She was already busy changing diapers and watching over the babies and fixing them small meals of scrambled eggs and milk-coffee filled with mushed-up *korppu*. Sophie Seraphina, the oldest, was her mother's two extra hands. Too soon she became, in addition, her mother's eyes.

Mr. Makela was useless, worse than useless, I often heard Äiti whisper to Isä in the nighttime secrecy of their double bed behind the curtain in the corner. She was right. Even I could see that.

During the hot, still, sun-baked days of summer when Isä had more to do than he had hands to complete the tasks—barn work and garden work, fields to clear, endless hours of work, Mr. Makela often appeared as early as mid-morning with a fishing pole in hand, asking Isä to come along just that once. "*Liian kuuma päivä,*" he'd grin, "too hot to work."

Isä would shake his head ruefully, for he too loved to fish, and the brook trout swam sweet and small in the creek past Seinolas. But Isä never went—even after supper—at least during the hours of daylight. Once in a great while he would run there at dusk with Tonttu at his heels and stay until the moon lighted his pathway home, the creel always full of silver slivers of moon-beam that Äiti pan-fried for breakfast. But mostly, he was just too busy to fish.

Small wonder that he had greeted the advent of Tonttu with some secret sense of joy. Tonttu had two strong and, we soon found out, very willing hands.

Within a few days of the beginning of his transformation into a civilized being, though still child size, he had taken over completely all of the small but time-consuming daily household support chores: splitting and carrying wood, cleaning the woodbox, carrying in water and hauling out slops, milking Dolly and cleaning out her muck, all before the work of the day began out in the fields.

Largely thanks to Tonttu, Isä had felled more trees, pulled more stumps, piled more rocks into windrows, planted more potatoes, built more fences than he ever had day after day before that summer.

In addition, he had begun to dig a well in the spot indicated by the water-witch. It could not be denied that Mr. Makela, for all his profligacy, had magic in his hands when he took hold of the two ends of the Y of a willow branch and held the central leg suspended over the ground. When Mr. Makela walked over a spot where water lay below the surface, the point of the Y dipped down. It would not work for any of the rest of us. But Mr. Makela had the magic in his hands.

In payment, Isä gave him one full day of work from all of us. Tonttu took over supplying their wood and water, filling every bucket he could find. Äiti and I attacked the cleaning and the piles of laundry mouldering in the porch. We directed Mrs. Makela to spend that day bathing her eyes in spring water and lying down in the cool quiet of the sauna porch, the dressing room, which we scrubbed first. Maija-Liisa entertained the children (a euphemism for playing) after we all ate a hearty breakfast. Äiti had fried bread dipped in egg batter and served it with butter and maple syrup and thick crisp slabs of bacon. Until she could freshen up the kitchen—that was another euphemism that made my eyes roll—until, in truth, she could shovel the filth out so we could find the floor—she cooked over the open fire that Isä had rigged up outside.

By the time we left that night, Mrs. Makela confided gratefully to Äiti—seeing (well, knowing) that the floors were scrubbed, the woodbox full, the dishes washed, the clothes dried and folded, the children bathed, and bread made—she felt comfortable for the first time in months.

It was not that Mrs. Makela was lazy, although that was the general neighborhood assertion. Sick as she was, she simply could not keep up. She needed more hands. Unfortunately, that was the one thing Mr. Makela was to provide with a will. All told, she birthed sixteen children, all but two of whom lived past infancy. She never saw the faces of the last eight or nine, and she blessed to her last breath the same fact that Mr. Makela cursed—that the first five had been girls.

At any rate, clearly, more hands helped.

Äiti always said, appreciatively, when Maija-Liisa and I were more than usually willing, "Many hands make light work." Comparatively speaking, it was true. Lighter anyway. Thus, when morning came and we discovered the note, we all grieved—

—Isä because he would miss Tonttu dreadfully. Pragmatically, he had increased our work force by one-fourth, but Isä had also come to care for the boy.

—Maija-Liisa because he had finished the corn-husk doll, which sat right by the note. But she had no way of saying her *"kiitos,"* her special thank you, words she was proud of having mastered.

—Äiti because she could never bear to have our circle of love broken, and that circle included Tonttu.

—I simply because my heart ached. Even now after these many years have passed since that morning, I find it difficult to express how I felt. I had come to depend on him, to lean on him like a brother, whether I wished to or not. I truly no longer blamed him for what he had done to Verner or for what he had said at Lake Leander. I had accepted the fact that there were forces at work in Tonttu and in the world that I could not understand. Moreover, I had recognized myself as fallible and feared the depths of that fallibility. In my own way I had been as vicious in my actions to Tonttu as had been his retaliation.

Someday perhaps I would be big enough and wise enough and strong enough to understand it all or at least to ask Äiti and Isä for help in understanding.

For that time then, however, I went on from day to day, filling the hours with work, mostly willing myself not to think, drawing a shade over my eyes like the one Mrs. Makela endured and escaping when I could into a world of imagination wherein all reality lay suspended.

I began to think up my own stories and in effect to live within them as I washed and ironed and scrubbed and cleaned and watched Maija-Liisa. I developed a world of my own, peopled with the Hölömöläiset, a world in which each morning they awoke to face dangers of unspeakable variety only to find themselves each night victorious.

It was an immensely satisfying world.

It too almost shattered when we found the note.

"I know that it is time for me to leave. Thank you," it said, simply. Tonttu, too, had mastered those words. We knew he meant them.

Tonttu had gone.

Where, we knew not.

Why, I knew. No matter how he tried, he had not been able to escape into a dream world like mine. He never could, never in his whole life. He always faced reality. And reality told him that he was culpable. He had hurt Verner. Obviously, he had dealt me an equally devastating blow. Fairness dictated that he make amends, not to Äiti and to Isä. He had tried in every way to repay them for their kindness. But to Verner. And perhaps, later, to me.

Thus, when we awoke one morning in early November to the first snow fall of the winter and the resulting cessation of seasonal outdoor work, it was to a peculiar stillness. No one was splitting wood. No one was stoking the fire. No one was grinding coffee. No one was trying to walk so quietly that the very quietness creaked.

The bedroll by the fire was neatly rolled. The woodbox was full. The fire was blazing on the hearth and in the woodstove.

But the sauna and the barn, too, it was soon discovered, were empty.

Reality shouted that Tonttu was gone. And his note confirmed the fact.

It broke my heart.

Chapter 15

"Hölömöläiset, Hölömöläiset"
Hölömöläiset Tales

I HONESTLY DO NOT KNOW how I would have survived that early winter time had it not been for the Hölömöläiset.

I often thought about running away, as Tonttu had, and in a sense I did. But my body remained within the confines of our small world. It was only in my mind that I left a circumstance that, had I not found escape, would have been untenable.

Sometimes when I thought about Tonttu and how unspeakably cruel he had been toward both Verner and me, anger still flooded the whole of my being. Then I was fiercely glad that he was gone.

But in the next breath, like the waves of Lake Superior breaking on the shore, the anger and the gladness were overcome with a lapping murmuring surge of almost unbearable grief. In a very real sense, Tonttu had become as essential to the workings of my soul as a stout keel and movable sails were to the workings of the Hölömöläiset ship. Without fastenings in the keel, the pieces of that cleaned-up pirate vessel, drifting into loose spars, floated off in every direction. So did I.

The conundrum of my feelings for Tonttu was compounded by the mystery of my own identity: was or was not Isä my real father? How and why had I come to be given the birth money? And what was it that had happened in Boston that Äiti could bear neither to remember nor to forget, choosing instead to hide the time she spent there in the leather-bound trunk, securely locked and fastened?

When my own attention had been centered on Tonttu, that concern had been set in relative abeyance. Tonttu gone, it crept out again, mostly at night, in the dark.

Thus, I did not, early that winter, ever really sleep as I had known sleep in the days before. Instead, during those dark hours of the night I faced the lurking mental monsters I called "maybes"—

Maybe Isä and Äiti had adopted me, maybe I was a foundling, maybe Maija-Liisa wasn't really my sister. Maybe I had no real family, maybe one day Äiti and Isä, tired of feeding me, would send me away. Maybe Tonttu, lost, alone in the woods, was cold, or wet, or hungry . . . or dead. Maybe the axe I had wrought with my anger had chopped away not just at his fingers but at his very heart. Maybe he would never come back and we would never find out what had happened to him. Maybe Äiti and Isä, somehow discovering the horrible things Tonttu and I had said to each other, would confirm that they all were true and admit not only that they didn't really care at all about Tonttu, as I had insisted, but that they did not care at all about me either.

Maybe, like Tonttu, I would always be alone.

Maybe I too should leave.

Then I did leave, nightly, departing physically from the warm spot by the curve of Maija-Liisa's back into a part of the bed that was cold enough to keep me awake, departing mentally to another world, another time, another identity. During the ensuing dark hours before Isä got up to throw fresh logs into the wood stove and the *kakluuni*, I found within me the strength to escape, to submerge my own reality into the mythical world of the Hölömöläiset.

Isä had set up an interesting puzzle when he accepted our simple solution to the disposal of the Stallos: none of the Hölömöläiset knew what the giant had done to the keel and the sails.

☽ ◯ ✸ ◯ ☾

Thus, NEXT MORNING, when, the problem of the Stallos ostensibly solved, they set about setting out on the long voyage to Amerika, two new problems presented themselves: the sails would not unfurl and the ship would not hold fast against the water. No matter how they tried, their bailing could not keep up with the inrush. No matter how they tried, the wind would not help them move the ship to shore. No matter how they tried to tie things together, the reconverted pirate ship had begun to crumble.

[*What an enthralling, all-encompassing, totally engrossing state of affairs! What a problem for me to solve! Best of all, it was a problem about which I could bear to think, one I actually enjoyed mulling over, one I pecked away at, night after night, as diligently as the chickens in the coop that Isä had made attacked the grain I threw for them morning and night, as diligently as I searched for their eggs.*

The keel was the first and immediate concern: who would refasten the spars and how? I did not have the answer.]

But Ahti Hölömöläinen did, Ahti the sailor who had sung the waves to sleep so the Hölömöläiset could get their winter stores, Ahti the sailor who had found his real home in the pirate ship.

"First, Eino the oldest, then Matti and Urho, then Toivo and Sulo, the twins, Onnie, Pekka and Kalle," called Ahti, the sailor, "and Severi, last of us Finns! *Tule hopusti!* Come quick! We have work to do!"

To Onnie he gave the job of finding strands of grapevine wreathing, dried in the fall, bereft of leaves.

Onnie jumped into the water and swam to shore and set off on his way.

To Eino and Matti and Urho, who kept their axes in scabbards by their sides, right next to their *puukkos*, he gave the task of chopping down the tallest trees that they could find and clearing off their branches to make new masts.

To Pekka and Kalle and Toivo and Sulo and Severi went the hardest job. They were to join hands, one to the next, to swim down around the loose spars of the keel, and to hold them together as closely as they could until the grapevines and the new masts arrived.

Father Jussi also had a plan, one that involved the girls, and the two plans complemented each other perfectly. He gathered Liisa and Toini and Suoma and Hilja and Florida around him, and whispered.

They clapped their hands when they heard his plan, delighted that they could stop bailing. Running to their hammocks in the hold, they dressed themselves in their very best clothes—hats, dresses trimmed in braid, silk scarves, leggings, and boots—and set off in the dingy, the oldest two manning the oars, all of them manning the mission, in a sense; for they had been directed, by Father Jussi, to enlist the aid of the pirates.

Now the Hölömöläiset girls, though young, were, like most Lapland women, truly lovely even in their workaday clothes. But dressed in their best, they veritably shone with energy and enthusiasm, red cheeks and sparkling blue eyes vying with the red and blue of their dresses and leggings.

The pirates, it was true, were not romantically inclined, as Father Jussi and the girls themselves well knew. They were far more interested in plentifully set tables than in meaningful relationships, and they concentrated their energies more on shanghaiing replacements than on searching for love.

So in addition to beauty, the Hölömöläiset girls needed attractions of a more concrete variety: ergo, food was to be found and temptingly prepared, and the Hölömöläiset boys were to be offered as bait.

"Here, pirates! Here, pirates!" the girls called, much as they had to the fish. Rowing along the shoreline, they coaxed, "Here, pirates! Here, pirates! Come and get some food!"

"Here, pirates! Here, pirates!" Their voices were alluring. "Here, pirates! Here, pirates! Come get the boys!"

Sulking after being outwitted by Father Jussi, for the cheese had looked just like a rock, and no rock could spurt liquid, the pirate chief and his men had withdrawn to an island just off shore where many Sami families brought their reindeer for the summer to escape the hordes of flying insects that formed black clouds upon the tundra and the unexpected heat that accompanied almost twenty-four hours straight of daily sunshine.

The pirates had masked themselves as fishermen; for they were, it was true, in total control of the fishing boats, having overcome the owners of the boats, forcing them into slavery.

Oh, they were cruel, those pirates!

But they were not as smart as they thought they were and definitely not as smart as the Hölömöläiset girls.

Reaching the shore of the island and beaching their dingy out of sight of the pirates' enclave, Liisa and Toini and Suoma and Hilja and Florida headed straight for the cache of food Father Jussi had hidden on the island to use that summer after they had swum their reindeer across the isthmus and onto the cooler, bug-free land where they had planned to spend one of the eight Lapland seasons. This was custom, not just for the Hölömöläiset family, but for all Sami families.

The pirates had known that, and known they could demand payment for helping the weaker, younger reindeer to swim the channel from mainland to island. They knew they could demand exorbitant payment, for the Sami families were rich in reindeer, and reindeer were rich in all that was needed for survival—milk, food, transportation, friendship, household goods and clothing, even housing, all walked latent on the strong hooves of those antlered animals.

In fact, most Sami families in Lapland with enough and to spare stored caches of goods in secret hidden places on the islands, ready for use in time of need.

Their need great, the Hölömöläiset girls dug deep under the roots of the pine trees just where Father Jussi had told them to dig and found . . . treasure! Reindeer meat, smoked salty and dry. Cheese, encircled by a tough covering, meltingly soft and mellow inside. And best of all, fermented reindeer milk, so powerful in its afterglow that the pirates would not know they themselves had been shanghaied until it was too late.

Sure enough, Father Jussi's plan worked.

The girls just had time to lay out the lavish spread before the pirates, tempted by their siren songs, appeared, hungry and tired from the unaccustomed toil of transporting reindeer and cleaning the fish their slaves had caught.

And before the half-light of nighttime slipped over the land, the pirates, replete, had fallen asleep.

Then the girls carried them, sleeping the sleep of the unjust and unwise, one by one, into the dingy. They rowed it back to the ship, which was

still mostly intact. They roped the sleeping pirates into one long row and dropped them down around the keel. The boys, grateful to be relieved of their task, woke the pirates up just in time to tell them it was their turn to hold the boat together.

The pirates were not pleased. But they did it, willy-nilly.

All this time Mummu Hölömöläinen had been taking care of Baby Vieno and thinking to herself.

Next morning when Eino and Toivo and Sulo came back with the new tree trunks, tall and strong enough to carry even the highest top-gallants and when Onnie came back with enough grapevines to tie four ships together and when Stallo's mischief had been corrected and the ship made whole again, she said, "I think we will take them with us."

The pirates, that is.

"Make it so," said Captain Ahti to his crew.

And they did.

Thus, the Hölömöläiset set sail for Amerika with a full crew aboard, with Ahti as captain, with a reindeer herd stowed into the hold, and with their hopes and hearts high as the fore and mizzen masts.

I usually fell asleep somewhere around that time, part of my mind still busy. I had to decorate the captain's cabin suitably for Father Jussi and Mummu. I had to help the girls to prepare dinner after dinner for the pirates, who were always hungry, and to sew sailor clothes for the boys who were learning the ropes, so to speak. And I had to invent ways for them all to entertain themselves during the long and dangerous voyage.

Suddenly it would be morning again.

Late that fall I was officially enrolled in school for the first time, grateful for the first time for the work Äiti had forced me to do on sums, aware for the first time of the potential to capture the butterfly wings of my dream-stories with a net of words. I learned not just to read well but to write.

That was to be my initial step toward salvation.

First, I wrote words.

Then I discovered that the dictionary was full of them, good words, better than "bastard."

Then I wrote whole sentences, putting the words together in infinitely satisfying ways, arranging and rearranging them, playing with them, as the other children did with the jigsaw puzzle pieces the teacher brought for us to tackle during lunchtime and recess.

And finally, to my infinite delight, I put the sentences themselves together in sequence, set them down for all time, permanently, on paper, not just with chalk on my slate, but with pen and ink neatly to last for all time.

My first composition was a letter.

I addressed it to Tonttu Victormaki, Wherever He May Be.

I asked him to come home.

I called it home, our house, his home.

I called him brother.

I called him home.

The teacher, Miss Maki, took it with her when she went home for Christmas break.

And lo and behold one cold night in January . . . when the frost had frozen the ruts on the trails so hard and firm that a team of horses could pull a sledload of wood, tree trunks piled higher than our house, for miles and miles through the forest to a mill site . . . when the lakes too had solidified into roadbeds as safe and secure as any land-bridge leading from here to there . . . then we heard the jingle of sleigh bells and the slithering of a sleigh whipping along the ice trails and the whoof and tramp of a horse pulling it smoothly along, and the sounds stopped right outside our door.

And there, praise be, stood the second Mrs. Victormaki, Titian hair flying from under her hat, and Verner, hearty and almost whole, and behind them both, Tonttu. Smiling.

He had heard me. He had come home. And he was never ever to leave us again.

Moreover, the three of them were not alone. Wrapped in a baby quilt, squirming in Verner's arms, was—not a baby—but a small, wriggling, snuffling ball of golden fur, mostly ears, nose, and tongue. A small dog. A puppy. Molly Honey. Tonttu's peace present to me. My final salvation.

Chapter 16

Home Again

NO ONE HAD AN INSIDE DOG IN THOSE DAYS. There was no extra food to give to an animal that did not work; there was no time to train or teach it. No one had pets. Cats lived in barns and killed mice. Dogs slept outside and herded cows. All except this dog. This dog slept in a box by my bed, and, when it awoke at night with a full bladder, I brought it—her—outside to tinkle in the cold. In between trips outside, I slept, increasingly deeply as the days and nights went by.

Tonttu, Mrs. Victormaki, and Verner stayed with us for as many nights as it took to reclaim the Victormaki house from the frost and freezing cold. Isä went with Tonttu the first morning after their return to start fires in the wood stoves in kitchen and living room, their frame house having four rooms, unlike our one, two up and two down. Heat rose gradually through the ceiling registers to the bedrooms upstairs. Both downstairs rooms were warmed by wood stoves, the one in the kitchen, a huge black Acme range for cooking, the one in the living room, a silver-plated heater with an isinglass door that opened along the high vertical front into a capacious firebox large enough to maintain a fairly constant temperature. Sooner than would have been possible with our *kakluuni*, the Victormaki house was reasonably warm.

Then Äiti and Mrs. Victormaki set to cleaning it. Of course, they couldn't wash the windows. Even when the sun beat directly on those that faced the south, the frost melted only in the middle and that only during the warmest part of the day. But they swept the cobwebs from walls and ceilings and beat every rug until the dust flew as hard and fast as a blizzard of snow. They scrubbed every surface, flat or carved, with the oil soap Mrs. Victormaki had brought from Soudan and washed knick-knacks, pictures, mirrors, and all other glass with ammonia water and vinegar.

Last of all, they put clean flannel sheets on the beds upstairs, having

109

aired the quilts and pillows and chenille bedspreads for a full day outside in the sun.

When all else was done, they set the kitchen wall clock to the correct time, as near as they could guess it, poked the pendulum high enough to ensure movement, and stood back to listen to its measured beat.

Although the Victormaki root cellar sat virtually empty and almost completely inaccessible, snow having blown hard against the doorway and never having been shoveled away that winter, we had enough and to spare for three friends to share, as Äiti said. Potatoes aplenty. Venison, canned, smoked, and frozen. Onions tied to dry and left to hang in festoons from our kitchen ceiling. Apples and carrots and rutabaga, the latter two dry-packed in sand in twenty-gallon Red Wing crocks.

Neighbors, seeing and smelling the wood smoke drifting up from sauna and house chimneys, led back the Victormaki's cows, three in all, so there would be milk and cream and butter. Every family sent some kind of starter too—for bread or *viili* or squeeky cheese.

Even without a man, it seemed Mrs. Victormaki and the boys would make it. They'd survive. More than survive, in fact. For, freed from the oppressive presence of Mr. Victormaki and from the multiple mouths of the younger Victormaki children, a sense of joy permeated the very texture of the house and barn and yard and sauna. Even the outhouse door swung more freely on its hinges, well-greased by Tonttu.

Everything moved to the songs Mrs. Victormaki sang. With or without the accompaniment of the *kantele*, music floated into and out of, around and about every corner of that homestead where it had never before felt free.

That winter Suutari Erkki had no reason to stray afar in search of Elysian Fields. They lay all around us.

Tonttu worked hard, of course. But he didn't lack for helpers. Mr. Victormaki gone, Mrs. Victormaki did not lack for suitors anxious to exchange their labors for the sound of a song or a smile from a pretty woman.

Oh, they never imposed. Her reputation remained intact with so many vying for her favors that she was rarely if ever alone with any one of them.

Suutari Erkki made shoe packs not only for the three of them but for all of us and everyone else around. He also made shoes and boots, singing away as he treadled his machine, "Toodle-um, toodle-um, toodle-um." And the Victormaki living room was, of course, large enough to house both machine and material, an ideal warm welcoming work area.

We watched him card thick bats of grayish colored wool shorn from the Hagglund's sheep, using wooden paddles with short metal teeth.

Then instead of spinning the wool into yarn as thin and even as Kastren Papa's store-bought yarn, he did what Äiti had warned me time and time again never to do when I washed our mittens and scarves and socks. She directed me to keep the water very cool and to lay the wet wool carefully on a flat surface, molding it back into its original shape carefully with my hands.

Suutari Erkki did the opposite, the unforgiveable: he wet the wool in hot water then laid it out in thin layers, layer upon layer, changing the direction, in thin sheets of gray matted one atop the other. When it was about a quarter of an inch thick, he molded it to the recipient's foot, working it higher than the ankle, then let it dry. At the top he sewed a single colored length of yarn over and in as a decoration.

Most felters stopped there.

But not Suutari Erkki. Not for Mrs. Victormaki.

After he had made the wool into felt and shaped it to her feet, he cut a thin leather sole the shape of her foot out of precious sun-dried moose hide, so soft it was possible to breathe through it, and whipstitched it to the bottom of the shoepack.

Then because like Äiti Mrs. Victormaki wanted everything that was functional also to be beautiful, he knitted a two-inch piece of yarn dyed with red onion around the top, tacking it in a bit at the ankle, binding it so it curved slightly.

Finally he added three decorative touches—first, swirls of evenly spun yarn forming a pattern atop the instep; second, a froth of softly woven yarn bearding the toe; and third, at the top, fluffs of carded wool weaving in and out of the ankle ribbing. The result was almost too beautiful to wear, even as house slippers.

Mrs. Victormaki thanked him so profusely that he disappeared for three days and returned only when we bribed him with rabbit stew and dumplings.

Then he made three more pairs for "the rest of my girls," for Äiti and Maija-Liisa and me.

Lehti Aapo snowshoed through the woods loading dead and fallen trees onto his homemade kick sled, and chopped them into stove lengths and willingly piled the lot. Mrs. Victormaki served him morning coffee at the round table in the kitchen, and pretty soon he claimed one thick white mug as his own, not to be washed until evening.

Kastren Papa trekked along the ice roads bringing news from town—none about Mr. Victormaki's whereabouts, praise be—and his coat was lined with needles and pins and ribbons and bright store yarn and floss for embroidery. Äiti set Maija-Liisa and me to making samplers to practice our stitches. Kastren Papa made molasses dosings for Verner, who drank them without demur, since they were accompanied by stories about pirates.

Even the Raihala boys forebore from knife fights, instead bringing their roly-poly, red-cheeked mother over for visits and hanging around themselves to dunk crisp cinnamon sugar *korppu* into coffee laced with sugar lumps and fresh cream rather than moonshine. Sober, they were nice boys, a bit uncouth and ungainly, it was true, but they meant well.

One of the older boys, Eero, taught Isä how to set a beaver trap underwater. Beaver skins, cleaned and stretched out, sold for as much as twenty-five dollars apiece at the trading post in Soudan. Isä made enough to replace some of the coins he had borrowed from my glove box of birth money.

It was a halcyon time, the days short but satisfactorily busy, the old routines recaptured, with Monday washdays and Tuesdays spent ironing, Wednesdays when the smell of fresh bread and blueberry pies made from canned blueberries wafted even to the Victormaki house, and we had three guests for dinner even though it wasn't visiting day.

On Thursdays we cleaned the house until it was spotless and ourselves too in the sauna, and we met every Saturday to dance and talk and play and every Sunday to sing hymns and say aloud and often to God and to each other that we counted our blessings and found them legion.

Every weekday morning after the daily chores were well on their way, I was excused to put on my skis and take my slate and my lard bucket filled with leftovers and speed the three miles to the Nestor Kutsi home where the teacher was boarding and classes were held.

Mrs. Kutsi had hung a curtain across one corner of the kitchen to give Miss Maki a private room, and the five Kutsi children, as many of the Makela girls as could be spared, and I sat around the kitchen table doing our lessons.

At noon we ran outside to use the outhouse and to play duck-duck-goose in the snow until Miss Maki came to the door ringing the school bell and we hurried inside again to recite our memory work—the times tables for me. And poetry.

Poetry. It made winter into spring. I could not get enough of it, swallowing great gulps of Robert Louis Stevenson's *A Child's Garden of Verses.* As a culminating activity for the last day of school in the spring, I recited not only Lincoln's Gettysburg Address but twenty-five of the *One Hundred and One Famous Poems* I had read in Miss Maki's own book.

"Abou Ben Adhem" was my favorite. But my rendition of "Little Boy Blue" left everyone, even Äiti who had heard it a hundred and one times before, in tears.

The prize was that book. I cherish it still, though it is now as faded and worn as the little toy dog that was covered with dust: "Time was when the little toy dog was new and the soldier was passing fair, and that was the time when our little boy blue kissed them and put them there," I declaimed, with feeling.

Our own little boy, Verner, for he became all of ours that winter, continued to be more frail than he looked. And we did worry some that one day his toys, too, would await the touch of a little hand, the smile on a little face, wondering what had become of the little boy blue who had kissed them and put them there.

But that winter he ate well and rested well, and he and Maija-Liisa played together every day, learning, in the process, their numbers and letters, although they were still too small for school.

Tonttu should have enrolled. Mrs. Victormaki urged him to. He wanted to. In fact, most nights when the chores were done, I taught him what I had learned during that day, and he did half my homework. Miss Maki said that was all right.

But a day spent with books and studies was a luxury he denied himself. He was too busy making amends. No older brother could have been kinder to a real younger brother than Tonttu was to Verner. In truth, he served more as father than brother, teaching and helping and loving and nurturing, offering daily reparation all the more precious because it came from his heart, though it was Isä's pattern he followed.

Äiti and Isä had been right about Tonttu; I, wrong. He did not have the soul of a snake. In fact, once when one of the bigger Kutsi boys, Art I think it was, scared me by throwing Molly Honey down the hole of our outhouse during a Sunday *kahvi kekkerit,* Tonttu not only got her out and cleaned her up but beat Art into a profuse apology and a promise never to bother me again. He didn't, either. And he left Molly Honey alone after that, too, for since we were always together, what happened to Molly Honey redounded on me, and vice versa.

She slept at the foot of our bed, like a hot water bottle against whom Maija-Liisa cuddled her cold feet. Much better than against my back and legs.

Molly Honey lay by my chair at mealtime, although always near Maija-Liisa, too, for she was still a messy eater. Molly was accommodating about scraps that fell onto the floor. Äiti and I never had to sweep them up.

On Saturday nights Molly Honey, too, went to sauna, and afterward I brushed her golden coat dry until it gleaned brighter than the gold pieces in the glove box of the trunk. She was far more precious to me than they could ever be.

And she was adopted. She wasn't born ours. Äiti and Isä and Maija-Liisa and I were not her birth family. But we were bound together by ties of love that superceded such limitations.

Äiti and Isä allowed her to follow them around while they worked and talked to her. Maija-Liisa flopped on her back and stroked her ears as if they were her cuddle blanket.

Verner and Tonttu and Mrs. Victormaki welcomed her to their house and tickled her tummy and gave her treats.

But she was mine; and I, hers. We were inseparable, joined together by invisible ribands of love.

And I, who was even during those happy days much given to over-analysis, sensed the rightness of it all even though I was not yet able to find the words to form that rightness into an articulated pattern. The sentences would not come.

When I read my thoughts in a poem by Edwin Markham, the north-ern lights spread banners across my horizon, and all other assignments lay in abeyance until I knew his words by heart, until I had, in fact, engraved them forever on my soul:

> *He drew a circle that shut me out—*
> *Heretic, rebel, a thing to flout.*

Tonttu had done that to me. I had done that to him.

We had erected walls and barricades behind which we had crouched, ready to flay and vilify anyone whom we perceived as a threat, even those who approached holding a flag of peace. As Tonttu had seen Verner as a challenger, so I had seen Tonttu and thence he had seen me.

We had drawn circles of black against each other then found our selves immured within their coils.

> *But Love and I had the wit to win:*

Well . . . not I . . . for sure.

I could take no credit, for I had been neither victorious nor wise. What I had seen as wit had in fact been witless.

The power that had finally broken down the walls, that had breached the barriers and undermined the outerworks, that had conquered our bleak and black fortresses did not, in fact, attack at all.

It bore no weapons, waged no war.

What it did was so simple, so artless, so lacking in artifice, so devastat-ingly easy, so uncomplicated and elementary that Maija-Liisa, small as she was, could already do it well.

And Äiti and Isä were past masters.

They knew the secret.

They had the key.

They used it every day, and they had passed the power on.

> *We drew a circle that took him in.*

Äiti and Isä had drawn a circle of love, and into their circle of love, they

114

had drawn us all—
>   —Lehti Aapo, Suutari Erkki, even Kastren Papa and Isotalon Antti,
>   —the Makelas and Verner and his mother and Tonttu,
>   —Molly Honey,
>   —Maija Liisa,
>   —and me.

We were together. We were one. We were safe. For no blizzard winds, no icy storm clouds, no wolves' teeth could break down the one impassable barricade that kept us inviolate: We loved each other.

As I thought about that one night after supper and sauna, I moved closer to Isä, moved there of my own volition, and laid my head upon his lap so he could smooth my hair.

I had not realized how much he too must have missed our closeness, for my braids did not completely dry that night even though the night was mild and the fire warm. Something other than sauna steam kept them damp.

There we sat by the fire that night long ago—Äiti and Isä and Maija-Liisa and me with Molly Honey spread out at our feet, her tail flapping now and again as if to say, "I'm happy."

So were we all.

Much later, when I was a great girl leaving home to go to high school in Mountain Iron to work for my room and board for the high school principal and his wife, saving my birth money for the dream of college, Äiti sat down with me and told me the facts.

She explained about Boston, about being an upstairs maid, about Charles Young, the scion of the family, young and handsome, about being paid to leave, about my birth in a box car on a railroad siding near the logging camp in Floodwood, about Isä's loving kindness.

But the facts, though important, did not change what was most important, then and always. What was most important, and what I already knew, was the truth.

During those difficult months at the end of my childhood, I had for a long time confused facts with truths, knowledge with wisdom.

I later learned that although those who seek knowledge can be satisfied with fact, those who seek wisdom must go beyond fact into a realm where reality and perception may, in fact, collide. For truth is composed not only of that which is evident to the senses but of that which is perceived by the soul. In that perception perhaps lies the difference between one who merely observes, catalogues, and reacts and one who makes a valid judgment.

What Tonttu had told me on that long-ago day at Lake Leander may have been—is—was—fact. I was not ever again, however, to mark it as true.

Truth defies the rational, the logical, the reasonable.

Truth cannot always be measured or charted or dissected.

It supercedes the power of humankind to interpret, sometimes even to understand.

It simply is. It is an absolute.

And upon that I came to place the whole of my trust.

That I might not be—was not—the child of Isä's body was fact.

That I was, nonetheless, forever and always, his child was truth.

Upon that and the strength of the love that bound us all into one, as truly as the Hölömöläiset, I could totally rely.

"Love is the doctrine of this church," I later memorized with a sense of profound recognition during confirmation class. "The quest for truth is its sacrament, and service is its prayer." Tonttu and I, confirmed together, recited those words together as we were later to recite together other words of commitment.

Truth, I came to understand, is far easier to feel than it is to express: it lies latent within, in a space that can be empty. But if love for someone, anyone, an Äiti or Isä or Maija-Liisa or Tonttu fills that void, a circle begins. And circles never end. That is the truth. That is all that matters.

And the Hölömöläiset . . . oh, they made it to Amerika eventually, but the journey . . . ah, that's another story.

Sometimes it is better to travel with hope than it is to arrive.

Except at the truth.

Glossary of Terms
Some Finnish, Some Finn-glish

Äiti - mother

ei - no

Elokuu - August

Haluatko kahvia? - Do you want some coffee?

heinäkuu - July, the month of haying (*heinä*)

heinä lato - a barn for hay

hopusti - used locally to mean "hurry up" or "hustle," although the dictionary
      says "*hoputtaa*" as "hustle" and "*hoppu*" for "hurry"

hyvä - Good!

Isä - father

iso - tall or large

istu - sit

jibbo - slang word for lumberjack

joo - used locally to mean "yes" and pronounced with a "y" sound

joo eli ei - used locally to mean "yes and no" (*eli* means "or")

Joulu Pukki - Finnish variation of Saint Nicholas or Santa Claus

Juhannus - Midsummer (*juhannus-päivä* - Midsummer's Day) - celebrated
      traditionally on the evening of the twenty-fourth of June

kahvi kekkerit - a celebration, generally an entertainment or feast, but in north-
      ern Minnesota, a get-together or meeting at which coffee and treats
      were served; in our community, a church meeting held at someone's
      house.

kakluuni - a heating place, perhaps four feet wide, floor to ceiling, made of
      brick or stone, possibly with an oven; a kind of fireplace but usually
      lacking the open fire box

kaksrivinen - a Finnish-American word for a *hanuri*, a small accordion

kala mojakka - a soup or stew made out of *kala*, fish

kalja - a kind of beer

*kamse - (may not be a Finnish word) term used for a Lapland cradle made of birch branches and reindeer skin

kantele - a small stringed instrument held on the lap and played with the fingers somewhat like a harp or a lute, a Finnish zither

kerma - cream

Keskiviikko - Wednesday

kiitos - thank you

kiuas - a sauna stove usually including both a firebox and a side area for heating water

*koftes - (may not be a Finnish word) a term used in Lapland for the dress of a Lapland woman

korppu - a rusk, a hardened crust of bread, often baked with cinnamon and sugar

lapsi - child

Lauantai - Saturday

lavat - benches usually built with several seating levels for sauna-goers, the lowest being the coolest part of the sauna, the highest bench the hottest area

Liian kuuma päivä - "Too hot a day."

Maanantai - Monday

Marraskuu - November

Mikä vaivaa? - What ails you? What's wrong? (Dictionary version: *Mikä nyt on hatana?*)

Minä sanon etta joku on hullu! - "I say that someone is crazy!"

missä? - where?

mojakka - a Finnish-American term for a soup or stew made of meat and vegetables

noki sauna - also called a savu sauna - a soot sauna or smoke sauna - bathhouse made without a chimney in the steam room, thus very smoky

No voi - a minor, rather meaningless expletive, like "Oh, Gosh."

No voi nyt piru - an expletive roughly translated, "Oh, the devil!"

omanpaikkasia - relatives or people from the same area of Finland

*pesk - (maybe not a Finnish word) a term used across the Lapland area for a loose caftan, an unstructured overcoat

piilu - technically a hatchet, used to mean a broad ax

poikatalo - technically a "boy-house" - in northern Minnesota, a boarding house, usually for single men

pulkka or *pulka* - a sled

pulla - sweet rolls, called "biscuit," often made with cardamom and braided

puukko - a small knife, specifically one used as a weapon

puuroa - warm, cooked breakfast cereal

Rakastan sinua - I love you

rieska - a flat, unleavened homemade bread, sometimes a round rather flat loaf of bread made without much or any yeast

sanoa - say

sattuu - in regional vernacular, a term used to mean "maybe" or "perhaps" or "it happens"

Se on puhuttu - It has been spoken. It is said.

silli salaatti - a salad made of herring and beets

*skaller - (may not be a Finnish word) a term used in Finland for reindeer-hide over-boots

sukulaiset - (from *suku* - family or kin) relatives or kindred

Sunnuntai - Sunday

Tiistai - Tuesday

Torstai - Thursday

tule - come

Tule hopusti - Come quickly

Tule tänne - Come here

tussu lakki - a regional term for a close-fitting knitted cap

tossut - house or bedroom slippers (*tossu* - a slipper)

tuuki or *duuki* - a regional term for a decorative doily or table covering, not a tablecloth or napkin, often crocheted

tyttö - girl

vetta (also *vesi*) - water

viili - a milk product like yogurt

Voi kauhia! - a mild expletive - *Voi* is listed as meaning "Oh!" or "Ah!" or even "Oh, dear!"; *kauhia* means "terrible," so the expression translates to "Oh, how awful!" or "How terrible!"

yo - yes, see *joo*

Sources

Halonen, George, ed. *English-Finnish Dictionary*, Superior, Wisconsin: Tyomies Society Printers and Publishers, 1924.

Wuolle, Aino. *Suomalais-englantilainen Sanakirja* (Finnish-English Dictionary), Ninth Edition, Helsinki, Finland: Werner Soderstrom Osakeyhtio, 1964.

*Words so marked did not appear in either source, nor were they familiar to the Finnish people with whom the writer grew up. The terms do appear, however, in source books about Lapland as a whole; therefore, it is possible that they are purely regional terms or that they are of either Norwegian or Swedish derivation.

Special Note to Finnish Language Specialists and Grammarians

Acquaintances who have been to Finland have often said that northern Minnesota Finns speak a kind of "canned Finn," based on the language as it was when their grandparents emigrated, much affected initially by their regional dialects and later by American influences, thus sometimes quite different from the purist's late-twentieth-century Finnish language.

It is the "canned Finnish" that my generation learned by osmosis, often from eavesdropping on grown-up's conversations.

Although I have made every attempt to use the Finnish language with respect, in instances where the dictionaries varied from what has been familial or common-area usage, I have opted to write the word as my parents and grandparents have used it over the years, according to the way my mother and her friends, second-generation Americans, spell it, trusting that such "northern Minnesota Finnish" can be accepted with grace as another element of a unique and very special oral tradition.

For all resultant errors of interpretation and usage, the author accepts full responsibility and offers sincere apology.